D1421080

That Which Doesn't Kill You

That Which Doesn't Kill You

CHRISTIAN THOMPSON

First published in Great Britain in 2002 by
Allison & Busby Limited
Bon Marche Centre
241-251 Ferndale Road
Brixton, London SW9 8BJ
http://www.allisonandbusby.com

A catalogue record for this book is available from the British Library

ISBN 0 7490 0553 X

Printed and bound in Ebbw Vale,
by Creative Print & Design

CHRISTIAN THOMPSON moved to West Yorkshire at an early age and attended Lancaster University. A qualified acupuncturist and masseur, he worked in the NHS for 8 years as a nurse and now works for Social Services. A cat-loving Aquarian, he enjoys cooking and is particularly fond of butter. This is his first book.

To all the people that helped the book along - you know who you are. Thank you. Special mention, though, to Mark Timlin for the inspiration and encouragement, Nick David for getting the ball rolling and keeping the beer flowing and to Cath and Katie for being there at the very beginning.

Chapter 1

Tim Marconi stood, legs slightly more than shoulder-width apart, hands clasped in front of him. Just standing there pretty much dead centre of my office rug. He had no need to be standing. I do have chairs for prospective clients to sit on. Three of them in fact. Some might call me over-ambitious.

I had motioned for him to take a seat, but he'd motioned that, thanks all the same, he'd rather stand. I surmised that Tim, being a nightclub bouncer by trade, was merely doing what he did best. Have you ever seen a bouncer sitting down? Me neither.

I must say he looked perfectly casual and relaxed as he stood there. Not quite as casual and relaxed as I must have looked, swivel chair tilted, feet up on desk. Of course, I'm not that déclassé with all my clients, but I know Tim and anyway, as long as you stop short of throwing up on them, bouncers tend to take a wide variety of manners in their stride.

Incidentally, Tim is only five-foot-three and would probably not have been particularly visible from my position had he actually sat down. Maybe the top of his shaved head. I'll also tell you that he was the least Italian-looking Italian I'd ever known. Tim wasn't his real name, but it suited him down to the ground. Maybe because it was short.

He was just coming to the end of the tale he'd been telling me.

"...so I haven't seen it with my own eyes. None of the lads have. So far it's just anecdotal."

I stared at him.

"What?" He stared back.

"A four syllable word? Are you sure you're a doorman?"

"Fuck off." We both smiled briefly, mutually impressed at our conversational prowess.

"And what do you feel I can do to help you, Tim?"

"Are you sure you're a fuckin' detective then?" Giving me a look that would have been bound to make most young lads drink up and scurry off into the night.

"Touché, Timothy. I suppose you want me to investigate these sordid goings on. Establish the truth or falsity of said anecdotes. Are you going to place any conditions on how I go about that?"

"No, I trust you. As long as you can go about it without upsetting my punters."

"Soul of discretion."

He nodded.

"And if I discover the rumours to be true?"

"We'll take it from there. Me and the lads will handle it."

"And if false?"

"Then we're all right, aren't we?"

"In a sense. How bothered are you at the fact that there are rumours in the first place? What could that be about?"

He looked like he hadn't even thought about that.

"I hadn't even thought about that..."

See. Detective.

"I suppose that opens up a whole new set of questions..." he said thoughtfully.

"Welcome to my world."

For falsehoods to become rumours they have to have a sustainable force behind them. An element of agreement is enough. If people want to believe the lie then it will become a rumour; social cohesion is promoted, the majority are happy. Gossip.

This was not gossip. It was not something that anyone would want to believe. Therefore it was either true, or there was a different kind of sustainable force behind it. Malicious intent.

"See what you can find out, won't you?"

"You might have to settle for 'balance of probabilities' rather than 'beyond reasonable doubt' but I'll be able to give you something." I was leaning forward now, forearms along the desk, shoulders hunched. Gone the nonchalance. Involved now. Conspiratorial.

"That's why I came to you rather than the police. So you'll get on it?" He gave a trademark grin. Slightly less soppy than Bob Hoskins.

"Yeah, I'll get on it."

So I got on it. My mistake. It wasn't long before I wished I'd left well enough alone.

Chapter 2

Tim's club, or should I say Mr. Trevini's club, was in town. So no travelling expenses on this one. Suited me fine. A smallish city like mine won't provide all the work an intrepid private investigator can handle so the job tends to take me pretty much all over the North. Liberal use of travel lodge rooms and the M62 tends to lose its appeal before long, so I was glad of the opportunity to work from home, even if it meant flat rate. I sat and thought about nothing much until the street lamps began to wink on outside the wet windowpane. Pale orange reminders that I had a home to go to and a cat to feed.

After locking up the office, setting the alarm system, and getting all the way downstairs I cursed myself, all the way back up the stairs, for leaving my mobile on the desk. I tried not to take it as a bad omen.

Tried not to let the traffic get me down either, drummed the steering wheel and pumped my clutch leg. The Bingley bottleneck was solid all the way back into Bradford. The same pedestrians would keep re-appearing alongside me outside the car window like extras in a low budget movie. At least I was dry.

Asda was heaving too. But I didn't care. I was in gainful employment and celebration came in the form of a multi-pack of Kingfisher beer. Bottles of course. Kingfisher only comes in bottles, and tinned beer is for the sad and the weak. By the time I reached the checkout my good humour was starting to vanish. There was a current fashion, at least round my way, for heavy woollen overcoats and garishly coloured fleeces. Add to that the relentless November rain outside and the warmth of the packed supermarket, and it was essence of wet dog. Also, I'd done that thing of getting a basket when, really, a trolley was required.

Back home, I cheered to the fine motor task of chopping

garlic and ginger. The cat had calmed down considerably after having been fed, but it was still wandering around with a thinly disguised air of criticism about it. It had a way of staring at me that seemed to indicate that I was doing something terribly wrong. I cocked my thumb and shot at it with my finger. It didn't flinch.

Having failed to get any fresh coriander, my intended curry had evolved into pork with capsicum peppers - a Sichuan favourite. The Kingfisher was now inappropriate. Good job I had a couple of bottles of Tsingtao in the fridge. I'm a bit of a sinophile - a lover of all things Chinese. I also make an effort to match my beer to my meals or to the occasion. If you think beer is just beer then may the Lord have mercy on your soul.

So. A person or persons unknown was/were, possibly, dealing drugs in Tim's club. Sorry, the club where Tim works. *Club Zed* - as it proclaimed itself in green neon. Now, drug dealing in a nightclub might not sound a big deal to you or me. But if you knew Tim you knew it was a big deal. Tim Marconi ran a tight ship, as they say. He didn't like being disrespected. No, I mean *really* didn't like it. Possibly an Italian thing. More than likely a height thing. He had a sense of humour, we busted each other's balls all the time, but you didn't want to cross him. Drugs weren't really the issue. He wasn't a moralist. It was the fact that someone thought they could get away with it. Well, they were taking the piss weren't they?

Bouncers are the 'gatekeepers' of whatever goes down inside a club. As often as not they are the dealers, or at least taking a cut. I sometimes work the door with Tim and the lads. I tell myself that it's to brush up on my observational and communication skills, but really it's when other work is thin on the ground. Tim thinks I'm a riot, he'd love me to be full time. I tell him my cat has expressly forbidden it. Anyway, the point is that I couldn't imagine any of the lads being involved. They wouldn't dare.

Going 'undercover' in the club was out of the question. Being a part-time employee I was a recognisable face. Playing the punter would look odd. Also, a single man in his thirties stalking round trying to score off anyone fool enough to speak to him? Well, I might as well tattoo 'I've got leprosy' on my forehead and have done with it.

So, I would work the door and the floor. I would be extra to the numbers so I didn't have to concentrate on watching anyone's back. The punters wouldn't know the difference. I'd keep my eyes and ears open and hope for the best. Cunning plan eh? You've got to start somewhere. If I was still clueless by next week I'd see the local pet shop about renting out a sniffer dog.

Thursday. I found out from Tim who would be working that night and got the numbers of anyone I didn't already have. Then I contacted each of them, right down to the glass collectors, to let them know what I'd be doing. I didn't want any animosity from staff who thought I might be investigating them. Course, I wasn't ruling anyone out but I didn't want them to know that. I'd make out we were all one big happy family. The very model of tact and diplomacy. Most of them I phoned but a few who lived close by I visited. Blag some coffee and biscuits. Also, any excuse to hand out business cards. It's a little distraction of mine to dream up rhyming couplets and print them out on cards. Most of my clients just get the one with 'Chris O'Brien Private Investigator' with my office and mobile numbers. Those who know me better get the quirky ones. I've way too much time on my hands.

Marsha was one of the employees I chose to visit. I've got to admit it was out of curiosity. She was a cleaner at Club Zed and the rest of us would joke about whether her legendary efficiency was down to pride or Obsessive Compulsive Disorder - we idly wondered what her flat looked like.

It was spotless.

No biscuits and the coffee had a slight hint of fairy liquid.

Marsha seemed somewhat agitated by my presence. I guessed that she was visualising the rituals she would have to perform upon my departure. Her eyes flickered from surface to surface that I had touched, brushed past or sat on, mentally disinfecting them as I spoke. I asked her if she had ever come across any drug paraphernalia whilst in the course of her duty - particularly in the restroom area. She responded in the negative. I asked her if she knew what a wrap was. She told me it was what I would be getting on my knuckles if I forgot to use the drinks coaster one more time. I drank up and thanked her for her time.

As I left I gave her my card. It was the one that said 'O'Brien Investigations - *Well educated and I rarely use force, all work considered except divorce.*' I checked her face for a reaction. Maybe the corner of her mouth twitched, but I couldn't swear to it.

My next visit was Large Benny. No real reason except that he was always good for a bottle of Dragon Stout. Today was no exception. The drink made up for the ordeal of having to pick my way through the refuse that was becoming endemic in that particular part of Bradford – the area between Manchester road and Little Horton lane that sloped gently uphill towards the Canterbury estate. A mixture of nightmarish council flats and Victorian back-to-backs separated by cobblestoned alleyways. Any rubbish that made it as far as a bin-liner would then have dogs, rats and pigeons to contend with. What attracted them in the first place was probably the amount of food waste that just gets chucked directly onto the street – primarily burnt rice and stale chapattis. But far be it from me to point a finger at any specific cultural group. Anyway, that wasn't the worst of it. Needles, wraps and ingenious pop can/biro combinations were a common sight – as were gangs of surly, hungry looking kids who hung around giving off the same sense of abandonment and displacement as the contents of a burst bin bag.

All in all, an unwelcoming place unless you knew a drink

was waiting for you. Not that Benny ever had any bother from the locals. Benny had wrists like Mike Tyson's neck and a neck that defied any attempt at simile. Hence the 'Large'. I'm sure you'll agree that 'Big' would be way too obvious an adjective.

Benny's sister had been a junkie. As a result he'd faced down some local dealers in the past, with not a little measure of success, I might add. She's been clean for a good while now. No stranger to the thousand yard stare, Benny could spot someone who was 'on one' a mile off. I asked him to keep an eye out and gave him the card that said '*I got style, I got class, but you don't want me on your ass*'. He threw his head back and laughed in short staccato oinks like Eddie Murphy used to. Some people had impeccable taste. As I was leaving he stopped me.

"Hey O.B., me and the lads thought one up for ya."

"Yeah?"

"Never lost an argument so cap him in a gunfight, he's a shitkickin' candy-ass bog-trottin gobshite."

Sweet. Love you too.

And so to work. The night began in true Thursday form. Quiet. It's all relative though. Zed is a popular club and could always pull a decent crowd. It just wasn't quite Friday or Saturday intensity. It was big, plush, well-appointed; pool tables and video games, a pleasure to work in. Hardly ever a hint of trouble on a Thursday. Perhaps it was because the crowd could afford to come out any night they liked, they weren't paid by the week. Yeah, Thursday nighters were like gentry. Add the fact that most still had work the next morning then no one was going completely mental.

To be honest, it wasn't the kind of place I'd go on a night out. Unless they were specifically having a 'hip hop' night or whatever, they still insisted on blokes wearing 'shoes' - didn't matter how shit they were, as long as they were shoes. I remember one night Danny turning some kid away.

"No trainers, mate." Danny said. Blank expression.

Glazed-over eyes. I jumped into the fray.

"Dan, those aren't just trainers. They're Acupuncture. They've gotta be, what, 130 quid?" I raised my eyebrows at the young lad.

"Ninety quid in a sale." He glowed with pride. Partly at the saving he'd made but mainly at the recognition I'd given him. Danny wasn't the least bit impressed.

"Still trainers. Move along please." Poor kid. He sloped off like a kicked dog.

"Like your Rolex too." Forty quid copy though it was. "Just tell yourself you're too good for this place," I shouted after him. Hey, permanent Rescuer Mode, that's me. Positive strokes cost nothing.

"I'm telling on you," said Danny.

I stuck my tongue out at him.

I thought about asking him if he shopped at Harvey Netto's but all I would have got was more blank expression. Or perhaps a beasting, later on, after he'd asked someone to explain it to him. Danny was an ex-para. I rest my case. I hear they land on their heads sometimes.

Personally, I tend to live in Vans or Converse unless work requires otherwise. If I'm door-stepping, particularly process-serving or repossession, then it's my trusty Timberlands.

The night continued to pass itself in unspectacular fashion. I kept doing the rounds, seeing and hearing nothing suspicious other than who was cheating on whom, who was getting fat, who had money to burn. Enjoyment, excitement, jealousy, anger, despair and quiet desperation. There are a million stories in the naked city. But tonight not one of them was drug related.

About half eleven I went out back and donned my rubber gloves - the kind with elasticated cuffs that you see bin men wearing. I'd purchased them specially for the occasion. I was out there to check the drain that leads from the bogs. Before opening time I'd lifted the cover and stuck some chicken wire down there. Purchased from the same place as the gloves, incidentally. I figured that it would catch most debris larger than sweetcorn. I won't tell you what was down there but there was nothing of any significance to the investigation. I planned on checking twice during the course of the night just in case it got really blocked. It looked like I needn't have bothered - all weight to my theory that the majority of people wouldn't entertain shitting in a public place - no matter how well-appointed.

The rest of the night passed without incident, unless you count a visit from an internationally renowned artist whose name I won't mention. Turner Prize winner. But seeing as most Club Zedder's didn't watch *The South Bank Show* he was just some twat with a ponytail. I went out to check the drain again after everyone had gone.

Nada. Zip. Niente. Nil Point.

All it told me was no one was flushing anything. It was unlikely that anyone would be daft enough to actually be using in there. I'd thought that maybe I might have panicked someone into jettisoning, but no.

I went back in and had my customary end of night Cognac. None the wiser. The sniffer dog might be a tad premature as yet. Perhaps another pair of eyes and ears might not go amiss, a more proactive pair at that. It was time to enlist the help of Kelp.

Chapter 3

Kelp was 21 years old but looked and acted a good few years younger. I'd met him about a year and a half ago and he'd perhaps matured a little in that time - maybe my influence. Kelp was the closest thing I'd ever get to an appreciation society. He started coming to the Kung Fu class that runs out of my local gym and managed to last for about one and a half sessions before the instructor canned him. He was a liability. That might sound a bit harsh to you but it was the right decision. Kelp, though brimming with enthusiasm for the martial arts, was the most physically uncoordinated person I'd ever met. So much for racial stereotypes. He had about as much coordination as a piece of spaghetti. Not much of a physique either - about as much muscle mass as, oh, say five or six pieces of spaghetti. Any decent instructor would have persisted with him if it wasn't for the constant Bruce Lee noises he insisted on making. Like a bizarre form of oriental Tourette's Syndrome. Basically, he didn't have *Noy Sing* - which roughly translates as 'The Right Stuff'.

Anyway, Kelp had stayed to watch me practicing on the *Mook Jong* and was transfixed. He hung around for me after the class and bombarded me with questions, eventually persuading me to come back to his place - well, his mum's place - and explore his collection of chop socky movies. When he found out I was a P.I. he almost shat himself with delight. A real wannabe. But he was good company for all that and, yes, it's sad, he wasn't at all harmful to my ego.

A couple of months after meeting him I helped him and his dear old mum with a spot of racial abuse they'd been getting off some of the neighbourhood. I mediated. No, really, I mediated. He was well disappointed that no fisticuffs were necessary. That's Kelp. Show him the moon and he'll only ever see the finger pointing. I've given up on trying to teach him stuff and he, bless him, has settled for being a kung fu anorak rather than a warrior.

From there on we'd hung out. Watched the odd fight film or ECW tape that he'd get from an American cousin. Whenever we got together he would drink cans of Red Stripe - a Roots Thing he told me - and I would drink bottles of Tsingtao. He calls me China. China O'Brien. If you get the reference then you probably watch too many fight films too.

Oh, and he's the only person in the world who I can beat at pool. Like I said, good company.

Now, Kelp isn't exactly my employee. I let him ride with me on occasion because it's good for his ego, and I guess I owe him that. No heavy stuff, and nothing he can really screw up on. He's actually becoming quite a decent observer. He might make an investigator one day. I seem to be scraping a living at it, so I do.

If anyone ever bothered listening to me, I would often remark that being a good investigator was 33.3% dispassionate observer, 33.3% fertile imagination, and 33.3% the ability to discern between the data from the first two thirds. I get a lot of blank expressions from people.

Morning. I awoke from a vague dream of being poked rhythmically in the chest by a grizzled prospector who then commenced drilling for oil adjacent to my head. Anyone with a cat will empathise.

I was suffering from that 'must try harder' feeling. Sometimes this feeling can be cured by going to the gym and literally trying harder. After my workout, it was debatable whether I actually felt any better. To do with the shower being broken I think. I'd have asked for a reduction in my monthly fee if I wasn't so damned polite. In between walking from the gym back to my car I managed to send Kelp a text message from my mobile.

U in?

By the time I was indicating out of the side street I'd been parked down my phone buzzed in reply. The traffic on the main road was still busy enough for me to read it at my leisure.

Like Flint.

It raised a smile with me. I had been responsible for teaching him how cool the likes of James Coburn were. Not to mention Michael - genuflect - Caine. I sometimes had to point him towards articles and reviews in *Loaded* magazine for back up before he was truly convinced.

On the way over, I stopped off at the sandwich shop and got myself a roast beef with onion and mayonnaise on white. I got Kelp the same plus a cream doughnut. He was young and skinny with a high octane metabolism. I sometimes worried that a crazed supermodel would defeat him in battle and eat his thyroid gland. I got a caramel slice for his mum too. No supermodel she.

He was the picture of gratitude when I got there and handed him his parcel. There's something primal about giving or sharing food. The 'Gift Relationship', anthropologists call it. Guaranteed to get you in someone's good books. Extrapolate anthropology to Crusty the street beggar or a woman on a diet and I find that you're on dodgier ground.

Kelp was as gracious a host as ever but the house seemed unusually empty and devoid of culinary aroma.

"Your mum not in?" I ventured.

"Correct." He stressed both syllables. "She's gone home for a whole month."

No wonder he was so glad for the food parcel.

"Oh, Jamaica?"

"Naa man, St Lucia. You know that!" He was genuinely incredulous.

God help us. Vaudeville had been murdered. The youth of today stood accused in the dock.

"Oh well, whatever. Never mind. You fancy some work?"

"Does the Pope shit in the woods?" One of mine, for sure. Hope yet.

I explained the deal to him. I would continue to work the door and the floor and Kelp would play punter. He had a natural demeanour of someone on E. All luvved up. Everyone's mate. Gushing garrulousness. He could circulate better than an erythrocyte. Hell, if I had drugs on me I'd definitely offer him some. Preferably Ritalin. He could report back to me on any offers he received.

We both thought the idea rocked.

We drove to the bank so I could get him some money. Money into the club; money for drinks; and a little extra to flash if he was on the verge of scoring. Got all my receipts. Wasn't sure yet if it was Tim or Mr Trevini forking out. I got the feeling that this was off Tim's back and that he wanted to get it sorted without Trevini's involvement. Made me wonder what price he was willing to put on his pride.

The price I put on my pride is, incidentally, 15 quid an hour. That's pretty competitive for investigative work. It's more than I was making as a nurse, less than I could make as an acupuncturist if I ever got my act together, but it kept the wolf from the door and petrol in the tank.

On the way back Kelp told me that his sister would be coming up to stay while Mum was gone. She'd just started the third year of a degree down in London at the School of Oriental and African Studies. She'd be coming home early for the Christmas holidays because his mum had impressed upon her that Kelp might need some looking after.

"Wait til you meet her, man. You'll get along. She can kick your ass too!"

Big deal. I'd never met a girl who couldn't kick my ass. I suffer from a bad case of Chivalry.

Chapter 4

"Thank God it's Friday' wasn't a sentiment necessarily expressed by nightclub staff. Town was busy. In order to try and hang onto to some of the clientele, the lesser clubs were doing cheap drink deals. It didn't much matter. Everyone who was anyone still wanted to end their night in Zed's. All it meant was that we ended up dealing with an increasingly disheveled crowd of hopefuls towards the small hours. We were the thin bomber-jacketed line holding back the ocean of strappy dresses and Ralph Lauren shirts.

I warned the door that Kelp would be on the scene tonight lest he had any trouble gaining entry. No one offered any comment but I got the impression that one or two were laughing up their sleeves at me.

We stayed pretty much out of each other's way. He seemed to be doing fine, not being too obvious. Just chilling. Some people he obviously knew from the way he was talking to them. I hoped he wasn't giving them any of the 'I'm undercover' routine. No, no one appeared to be laughing their ass off at him.

A bit later it was rubber glove time again. If at first you don't succeed. The cold autumn air bit at my face as I hefted the drain cover. My heart went out to the poor underdressed souls queuing round the front of the building. But hell, they were drunk, they could take it. Maybe hair gel has insulating properties. Who knows?

I scooped up the chicken wire. This time I had the feeling there'd be something.

Lifting the metal grid to eye level I studied hard. Rivulets, then drops, then drips of water fell back into the inky blackness of the drain hole. Drizzle from the skies dampened my hair. Why couldn't I see anything? Because there was nothing to see. Why had I got that 'feeling'?

Then I realised.

It was the feeling I was being watched.

You feel it on the back of your neck between the acupuncture points *Dazhui* and *Yamen*. The length of the cervical vertebrae. If you get it suddenly then it makes you whip your head round. This is a survival mechanism, which is good, but it also gives the appearance of being deeply uncool if you are only being watched from a distance - as opposed to facing an immediate physical threat from the rear.

I kept my cool. Replacing all the drain business. I kept my eyes moving without making obvious head movements. It was a long dark alley with lots of doorways, fire escapes, wheelie bins. Nook and cranny land. I thought about getting back into the building and finding a vantage point. I quickly discarded that idea as non-viable, estimating that I'd only be able to see about a quarter of the alley. I was in the alley now, why give up ground? Perhaps my watcher was up in a window themselves. Perhaps there was no watcher. Perhaps I was a twat.

I decided to brazen it out. If there was someone there it wasn't necessarily anything to do with the investigation. Maybe an adoring female fan. I walked the length of the alley and back, scanning everything with my Mag-lite and whistling Elvis Costello's 'Watching the Detectives'.

No one applauded or laughed or stepped out from the shadows.

I went back inside.

I had a brief exchange with the lads who had just been on the door as to whether they'd seen anyone coming or going down the alley. No. To be honest it wasn't the kind of thing they'd have been concentrating on and they'd have only seen one end of it anyway.

About three quarters of an hour later Nils - he's Danish - told me I was wanted on the phone. I told him it was most likely a talent scout who'd been watching my work recently.

"Just answer the phone, O.B.," he said and walked off.

These Europeans have trouble with our sense of humour, bless them.

I went into the office antechamber and picked up the handset that was lying in wait for me.

"O'Brien..." I stated.

"You were being watched," came the reply before the line went dead.

Sinister. Male voice. Well-spoken with no discernible accent. Emphasis had been placed on the word 'were', as if doing me the favour of confirming my suspicions. There was an impression of smugness, and I felt certain that the speaker had been the watcher. If I caved in to paranoia, I'd believe they'd heard that talent scout crack too.

It had sounded like a pay phone. It would have been stupid to call from anything else. There was every reason to assume that they were no longer in the alley, but that's where I was headed for, as quick as you like. Maybe I could find some physical evidence: footprints; a still-smouldering cigarette end of a distinctive brand; a book of matches with a hotel address on it. Detective stuff.

Nothing could have prepared me for what I found as I scudded out onto the wet tarmac.

A lifeless human body lay on the ground across the drain cover.

I wasn't qualified to pronounce someone dead but you will know 'lifeless' if you ever see it. Complete absence of movement. Not even the little ones that we don't even realise we see until they're not there. Stillness like you wouldn't believe.

A young man, dressed for a night out. Blood on his shirt and in his hair. A large contusion on his temple, a split lip. The light mist of rain was only just starting to dampen his clothes but the blood looked dry. I knew full well he hadn't been here an hour ago. I guessed he'd only been here a few minutes.

I knelt and palpated for his carotid pulse, turning my head away as I did so. Hopeless. Sirens were in the distance and getting louder. I decided the smartest thing to do was stay exactly where I was.

A squad car rolled up one end of the alley and a Black Maria up the other. Officers piled out of both. The ones from the van were in Kevlar vests.

"He's dead," I shouted "Careful where you walk, you'll want to seal this off for evidence."

"And who the fuck do you think you are!" shouted a tall man with luminous waistcoat and sergeant stripes.

"Err, under arrest?" I spread my hands.

"Dead right, mate."

Chapter 5

Things were chaos for a while as it seemed like no one knew where to put themselves. They knew where to put me though - in the back of the van, on the bench seat between a couple of officers. Those two seemed as shook up as I felt. The officers weren't very chatty so I took the time to do some deep breathing. Soon I could feel my heart pumping less and my muscles relaxing. I can never, however, quite manage the 'clearing your mind of all thoughts' bit.

With the side door open all I could see was a brick wall, a fire escape and an assortment of bodies moving briskly past in either direction. I could hear various sounds so my mind worked at filling in the gaps. The world and his dog were out there: Paramedics; CID; scenes of crime personnel; more uniforms; more vehicles. I heard a gruff voice mutter "Bloody vultures!" from somewhere behind the van, so I presumed the press must have arrived too. Made me wonder how many other phone calls Mr. Sinister-voice had made. Further away but unmistakable, I could hear the noise of disgruntled punters being sent home. It sounded like the uniforms were doing the job rather than the lads as there was far too much lip being given. Eventually they sat another couple of bewildered door staff in the van with three more officers.

Sergeant stripes stuck his head in and glanced round. None too pleased. I guessed he wasn't happy at the three of us being sat together but I think he just wanted us out of the equation by then.

"No talking," he barked before sliding the heavy door shut.

We had to stop twice for vehicles to move themselves before we were out of the alley and away. We stopped for surprisingly little once we were on the road.

We arrived via the Bridewell and up to the interview

rooms. It was a trip I'd made a few times before but normally through the front door and never under arrest - often as an 'appropriate adult' on someone's behalf, although there were plenty who'd tell me I was neither of the aforementioned. I wondered at first why they hadn't just kept us for interview at the club but I realised that would have been a nightmare for them. I guessed that they pulled all the door staff, with me as prime suspect, and would be questioning all the other staff on site.

They put me in an interview room with one officer for company and another outside the door. I think they'd sussed by then that I wasn't going to be anything other than cooperative. I was expressing this via my silence, so far speaking only when spoken to. Not surly, mind. A decent amount of eye contact, the odd smile here and there.

It looked like they were waiting for CID to interview me. I could wait. I didn't smoke, wasn't thirsty, didn't need the toilet. I was getting a little warm though, so I removed my Schott and hung it on the back of the chair. I sat back down and got on with some more *Qi Gong* breathing. The full exercise includes a horse stance and arm movements but I assumed that the constabulary weren't ready for the spectacle. Probably end up being seen by the police surgeon.

After about a million zillion years, and one change of officers, a young plain-clothes guy came into the room. He told me my lawyer was busy representing other Club Zed detainees.

My lawyer? How grand.

I told him it didn't matter, get on with it anyway. It was what he wanted to hear.

The guy sat down opposite to me across the table, switched on the tape, announced that he was Detective Sergeant Philip Hadley and that the interview was commencing and said, "So, tell me."

So I told him.

Right from Tim hiring me to the police turning up. As far

as I was concerned there was nothing to hide. When I told him about the anonymous call his ears pricked up but he tried not to show it. I didn't tell them about Kelp because I considered it irrelevant and I also didn't think they'd be interested to hear about how pissed off my cat was going to be when I got finally got home, so I let it ride.

When I finished he said, "So let me get this straight..." And we started again.

That's how it goes. Repeat the whole damn thing with him chiming in every now and then with suggestions that I was changing my story, seemed confused, was out-and-out lying - that kind of thing. A pleasure to watch him at his work. But his heart didn't seem to be in it. I hoped that by now they were forming the opinion that the guy had been killed earlier and dumped. It was what I believed.

The uniform from outside the door popped his head round and motioned for Hadley who went over to him and had a brief word. He looked back over at me.

"Your brief's here to see you. I'll be back."

And with that he left. Bye-bye Mr. Schwarzenegger.

So in walked my lawyer. Courtesy of Mr. Trevini I presumed. I glanced at my watch. 4.48 a.m and this guy looked fresh from the tailors. Platinum blond hair, silk tie and whiffing of Dolce & Gabbana. I was impressed.

"I'm impressed," I said.

I speak my mind if I know I'm not going to get into shit for doing so. Plus when I'm drunk - but don't we all? He offered me his hand.

"Thank you, Mr. O'Brien. I'm Steven Bateson Jnr." Robertshaw, Bateson & Penge. Mr. Trevini's lawyers. He was the son of one of the partners and had drawn the short straw. It was a big firm though, so I reckoned we ought to be honoured at getting this guy.

"I'm sorry I took my time. They would insist on interviewing the others first and they all wanted someone present."

I nodded.

"I gather you've already been interviewed. You didn't want to wait for me?"

"No offence. I just wanted to get on with it." I smiled as winning a smile as was possible at that ungodly hour.

"I have another colleague with me, and two at the club I might add, but I wanted to save you for myself."

"Charmed, I'm sure."

He smiled. Far more winning than mine. I liked him. Now, I like everyone but he was a breath of fresh air at this stage of the proceedings. Smart, well-spoken, with more camp than Butlins. Not many policemen you could say the same about.

I told him what I'd told Hadley. It was his impression that no charges were going to be pressed at this time. He told me that Trevini hadn't know about my investigation until the shit hit the fan tonight. Tim had actioned it himself but now it was all out in the open and Trevini would like me to visit him ASAP and discuss things. I said I'd get on it as soon as I had left the station and been to feed the cat. Steven told me that that would be super and asked me what I would suggest Mr. Trevini serve for breakfast. What a guy.

We discussed the fact that the police were unlikely to be forthcoming with any information that might pertain to my investigation but I asked him to keep in touch with anything he was able to learn. He said that he most certainly would.

I reached into the inside pocket of my Schott and pulled out a business card. Under the circumstances, murder and all that, I gave him a straight one.

He read it and said nothing, but when he glanced up at me he gave me a disappointed look.

I gave him puzzled.

"Your reputation precedes you, Mr. O'Brien. The office has told me about your cards."

Of course. Because of the Trevini connection I'd been offered some leg work from Robertshaw, Bateson & Penge in the past. I fished for another card and proudly handed him the one that said *'With a heart that's pure and a mind that's quick, if you pay me money I'll be your dick.'*

He did that thing with his nostrils. Think Kenneth Williams or Graham Norton.

"Steve, it's been a pleasure. We must do this again some time." I laughed.

"The pleasure's all mine Chris, I await with baited breath."

"And I, Steve, shiver with anticipation." Camp as you like.

I folded my arms and tilted my chair as he left. Chris O'Brien - if it moves I flirt with it.

Hadley was back before long. As well as his notebook he had some other papers with him. I figured it was getting near statement time.

"So. Private investigator, eh?" he said thoughtfully.

I didn't need to give him a business card then.

"Got some information on you." He waved the papers he was carrying. "You were involved in recovering that museum stuff back in April, weren't you."

"I think the word you were looking for was 'instrumental' rather than 'involved'."

Credit where it's due. I happened to kick ass on that particular case.

"But don't go thinking it makes a jot of difference with us, cos it doesn't, right?"

For the first time I noticed his faint Brum accent. Maybe the copper role was slipping and he was becoming more himself. He glanced back at the papers.

"It says here you've got a degree in Philosophy and Sociology."

I shrugged. "Proves nothing."

Got a smile out of him. Just a flicker, but it was there.

"Private investigators tend to be ex-job. You used to be a nurse. What's the story?"

"I like to help people."

"You should have stuck to giving bed baths, Florence."

"Wasn't much call for it, I was a psychiatric nurse."

"Proves nothing." He shrugged.

Touché. He was dead right. And he got a smile out of me.

He scanned the papers as if he was looking for more things to throw at me. I got the impression he was just curious. Maybe the first time he'd had a real life private eye sitting in front of him. It happens. As full and varied as my life is, my current profession is the most interesting thing about me. Breaks the ice at parties and in interview rooms.

He then placed in front of me the statement that he'd constructed from our taped interview. We went through it. It was fair enough. I signed it.

"We're letting you go, we don't like you for it."

If I thought he was going to thank me for my time I'd have a long wait.

"Best of luck. It's looking like murder rather than manslaughter, isn't it?"

He gave me a long hard police stare.

"I'd warn you against getting involved in this. Leave it to the professionals."

"You got a tip-off, didn't you?"

"Are you listening to me?"

"Check the phone you got it from, public phone, they'll be another call - to the club, the call I took. Maybe even a call to the press. All from the same phone. One after the other."

"O'Brien..."

"Whatever happened here was planned. It's to do with the club. Far be it from me to step on your toes but I doubt this is the last we'll be seeing of each other."

"Get out," he said. Tired rather than angry.

So I got. 7.14 a.m as I left the station. I'd like to say I was blinking in the sunlight but only because that would have been nice. This was November and it was still pitch black. It had dried up though. I shoved my hands in my pockets and sat on a low wall whilst I waited for my taxi.

My mind drifted back to the body in the alley. I knew then

that all my breathing techniques and all my wisecracks had just been pushing away that stark image with all the doubts, insecurities and horrors it stirred up inside me.

The sun would be up in an hour or so. Something that poor bastard would never see again.

Chapter 6

The taxi took me back to the club so I could get my car. I took a cursory look around the corner but the tape was still there and so was a crime scene van. Waiting for daylight, see if they'd missed anything. No chance of anything being left for me to detect.

I fired up the engine and headed for home.

As soon as I got my key in the front door the cat started in at me. High-pitched bugger. I petted it for about a quarter of a second then went and upended the remainder of a tin of Whiskas into its bowl. You get select cuts in gravy rather than in jelly, you can do that. Saves on forks.

It purred loudly as it ate. What's all that about?

I went upstairs to get dressed. I showered for fractionally longer than I had petted the cat then changed into Levi's, a hooded Mambo top and my Converse. No lawyer, I.

Before I departed I spent about thirty-two seconds making a fuss of the cat. It acted like it didn't want it. I told it that this might be all I had to give for a while.

It was a fine autumn day for a change. Auburn, green, grey and brown blended into each other as I drove at exactly 50-miles-per-hour round the outskirts of Ilkley moor. Law-abiding citizen.

I wasn't particularly tired now. Plenty of surveillance work and, before that, night duties had hardened me. I was used to the ebb and flow of fatigue. It didn't bother you if you didn't let it. That's what I told myself.

Mr. Trevini lived up on one side of a wide sweeping valley that was home to the River Wharfe. It was an area where lots of business people, executives and TV personalities had made their homes too. On a clear day you might see Richard Whiteley popping out for the papers. It's round about where the Pennines blend into the Dales and you start to see almost as much limestone as millstone grit. There were a variety of houses along the same road. All very distinctive. All very grand. Trevini's was hidden from the road by a millstone grit wall in which each stone had been sculpted then placed together dry style. The structure was old enough for a good deal of lichen to have become a kind of natural cement. Tall rhododendrons peeked from behind. If you were there in the summer, the smell of wild garlic was almost overpowering. Lush. All in all, not a good area to live if you couldn't afford extensive damp proofing.

I turned into his driveway. It's one of those semicircles that would take you back onto the road further down the hill if you kept driving. His Maserati saloon was outside the house rather than in the garage. Tim's Alfa Romeo parked behind it. These Italians.

I pulled my Escort in behind them both and hoped I wasn't letting the side down. The house was red brick, red tiles, oak doors and climbing ivy. Not exactly fair Verona. No balcony.

Before I could get to the front steps, there was a commotion from round the side of the house and a reddish-brown Staffordshire bull terrier came barrelling across the gravel and leapt at me.

I twisted and dropped to my right into *jor mah* - a sitting horse stance where most of your weight is on the back foot. The dog sailed past me at waist level. Who's bad?

Triumph was short lived though, as I was soon being licked almost to death.

"Yoda! What it is?" I fussed over him. Nice to be remembered.

He made some dog noises. 'Snarf' was one, another sounded like 'bartle'. He offered me his belly.

The front door had been left ajar for me and I walked straight through to his office/study/ library-type room. My history with these guys is that I met Tim Marconi in the gym and was offered occasional door work. I'd seen Trevini once or twice at Zeds and finally gotten to meet him when I signed

37

on to do some undercover work in one of his restaurants where some stock was going missing. It was a case with a satisfactory outcome, particularly as I'd also learnt the finer points of a good *Dolcelatte* sauce. Every Sunday throughout the summer, Trevini would host a barbecue - or 'cook out' as guests liked to call it - to which any of his employees were invited. I had made it to every one that I possibly could. Good food. Great atmosphere, everyone pretending to be a wiseguy.

They both stood as I entered the room. I nodded at Tim and put one of my hands out for Mr. Trevini to take. I wasn't sure what the mood would be but he pulled me into one of his masculine back-slapping hugs. Good job I'd showered.

They both looked knackered.

"Thank you for coming. We have things to discuss, Chris. Evie will prepare breakfast while we talk. What would you like?"

Evie had already been busy, as I could smell freshly baked bread. It would be *pain rustique* and she would have used French flour. Evie was French. Multicultural Wharfedale. She was also the maid. French Maid. No, she didn't wear the costume.

"I'd like to cook. May I?" I smiled.

They both smiled back and we walked through. They had trouble keeping me out of that kitchen whenever I was there.

Evie was pleased to see me. We air-kissed like they do on the Continent or in Chester. She giggled. She was 25 years old and looked like Liv Tyler. I wished she did wear the costume.

I hadn't seen Tim since Wednesday. He must have got to Zeds after I was pulled. He works in different locations but Club Zed is the jewel in Mr. Trevini's crown so he's there a lot. When he's not, he's travelling around various lesser clubs and restaurants. I guess you'd call him Head of Security or something. Trevini's right hand man. You have Tim standing at your right hand, it's going to make you look tall.

As I got the ingredients together Tim showed me an early edition of the *Telegraph*. 'Body Found. Nightclub staff quizzed'.

I read the article. It had about as much literary merit as my police statement. I shrugged and picked up a Sabatier.

At home I use my Kwangchow cleaver or my Global chef's knife - which is Japanese. But this was Evie's kitchen and I was paying homage. This was a French breakfast.

"Overcome with emotion, so he chops onions," grinned Tim.

Between them they told of the night's events from their point of view. They had been called in at midnight and had finally left the club around 6.30 a.m. It transpired that Trevini had not known about the drug rumours and me being hired until tonight. Tim had tried to get it all sorted out without having to worry him.

"You've had enough to worry about lately, Loz." Loz. That's what Tim calls Mr. Trevini. Lorenzo Trevini. No one else calls him that. Perhaps Tim has a need to keep things short. Like I said – a height thing.

"Perhaps you should tell me about your other worries," I ventured. The onions sizzled and browned in butter as I mixed the bouillon.

Things had apparently been going awry at various of the Trevini establishments over the past month or so. Anonymous but seemingly sincere letters to local papers about poor service received, anonymous tip-offs to environmental health. Vermin turning up in kitchens with previously unblemished hygiene records. Maybe not such a big deal until you added them together. But killing someone? This wasn't just someone who'd been ejected from a club or who'd had to wait too long for a spaghetti carbonara.

"Someone's really trying to yank your chain Mr. Trevini. Do you have any enemies?"

I crushed green and black peppercorns with a pestle and mortar and he shrugged.

"Why would I? A legitimate businessman? I have never harmed anyone."

It was easy to believe. He was a nice guy.

Evie had rustled some wild boar and apple sausages from the back of a cavernous freezer and given them a quick blast in the microwave, which you could tell she wasn't happy about, but now they were grilling nicely.

I added a dash of brandy and the soup was ready. *Voilà*.I sometimes add ginger for an oriental twist - but I was on my best behaviour.

We all ate, Evie with us, and talked some more. I told them what I thought. I told them that there seemed to be little substance to the notion that drugs were circulating in the club - but there were rumours nonetheless. There was purpose, orchestration, behind all of this. The anonymous phone call was a clear indication of that.

We all agreed that a dead body had taken this affair to a horrifying new level. If this were some sort of gangland turf war, then you might expect Trevini's employee's - or even family - to be targeted. We had all seen violence borne out of passion, out of a sense of violated honour. Yet this corpse appeared to be, so far as we knew, that of a stranger. The body, formerly a human being, had been dumped in the alleyway. As far as we could tell, with no higher purpose than to sully the reputation of the club. We all considered it somewhat of a step up from planting cockroaches or writing snotty letters. The cold calculation of such an act was truly chilling.

The club would be closed tonight as a mark of respect and out of sheer practicality for the knackered staff. The loss would be somewhere in the high thousands but no one mentioned it. It might not open for the rest of the week. They wanted to keep me on the case - whatever the case actually was. I told them I wanted to find out about the dead guy. They said that was fine.

I went home and fell asleep in the chair watching *WWF Livewire* on Sky One.

I woke up again around six. Watched the *Simpsons*, had a takeaway pizza and a bottle of Pinot Noir and then went to bed for real this time.

Chapter 7

Sunday. I checked in at my office. There'd been some post but only bills and junk. Only two messages on the ansaphone. Both from ex-clients, no offers of work; one little old lady asking me what I was doing for Christmas and one guy who was telling me that he had decided to become a P.I. and where could he go and train. In your dreams, buddy.

Maybe my ansaphone message was scaring potential clients away. I played it back. Me saying: "You want a Detective? You've found the right place! For a reasonable fee I'm on your case...".

Naa, couldn't be that.

Oh well. My dream of going to Cuba for a month to point a camera at a foreign businessman would have to remain in the realm of shadows.

I phoned Kelp. He'd texted me yesterday but I hadn't bothered to answer.

"Waass up ma nigga?" I enquired brightly.

"Yo dick!" was the retort.

"Was earlier, but I dealt with that before getting out of bed."

"What's on your mind, Bro?"

"Pub lunch." Actually the whole dead guy thing was on my mind and I was sure it would be on his too. But I didn't want to get into a co-counselling session over the phone.

"If you drivin' and payin'."

"Love it when you play hard to get," I said and hung up.

On a hill between Bradford and Halifax there's a place called Queensbury. It has two pubs both called The Old Dolphin. What are the chances of that? We lunched in the better of the two.

I had roast beef. Kelp had chicken. We both had all the

trimmings. I had Timothy Taylors Landlord and he had Stella. Afterwards, Kelp lit up a Marlboro and I had one too.

Did I say I didn't smoke? Never my own. I've been told I 'smoke like a girl'. So what? Recent statistics appear to suggest that girls are becoming rather good at it.

We both told each other our tales from the Friday night. Just the facts, or thereabouts. Kelp was buzzing with it, so proud to be involved. In his opinion, the rumours could not have involved anyone local. Kelp felt sure he would have found out something. He kept having to stifle his enthusiasm, reminding himself that someone had been killed. I saw him checking my face for approval at times. When I'd finished listening to him, I took centre stage for the final analysis. That's how we do it.

"I think someone's trying to damage Trevini's reputation," I pronounced.

Then I went on to tell Kelp about all the other shit that had been happening.

"I think I agree," he said wisely.

"I'm pretty sure there's more than one person involved. Difficult to dump a body on your own."

"Unless you're some seven-foot dude like Kane or the Undertaker."

"Hmm. Dude like that shouldn't be too difficult to detect."

"Be difficult to take down though."

"True."

I made a mental note to get back to Tim. Find out exactly when all these different nefarious events had occurred. Look for patterns. Had any occurred too close together temporally and too far apart geographically? Rule out lone seven-foot nutter theory.

"The other thing bothering me..." I took some of my pint.

"Is?"

Ahh, beer.

"The phone call I got. It seemed calculated to get me back out in the alley."

"So they were watching you?"

"Yeah. I know they were watching me. They told me they were watching me. What I want to know is how did they know to ask for me?"

"You figure someone on the inside? Someone who knew you were investigating?"

Kelp was all wide-eyed excitement now. I pulled my mobile from its carry case. Good. I had Nils in my phone book. I rang him.

"Yaas?"

Good. He was in.

"Nils! How are you?"

"I am well. Enjoying my Sunday. How are you? I can hear you are in the pub."

"I'm super. Thanks for asking. Nils, when you got that phone call for me at the club on Friday, what did they ask you?"

"They asked for you." He sounded confused, but then English is his second language.

"No, I mean, did they just say 'can I speak to the impossibly handsome blond guy who was in the alley just now' or did they say 'can I speak to Chris O'Brien' or 'O.B.' or what?"

"The policeman did ask me this."

"I need to ask you too."

"They asked for speak with Chris O'Brien."

"Nils, thank you. I've had a word with Odin and he says you're a dead cert for Valhalla."

He laughed.

"I speak to Jesus and he say you are asshole, O.B." He hung up.

"What did he say?" enquired Kelp.

"Jesus says you're an asshole, Kelp."

We were silent for a time whilst he appeared to consider the spiritual ramifications of this news.

"Inside job," I said eventually.

"What now?"

43

"I'm going to try and find out what I can about the bloke who was killed. Partly to see if that will tell me anything about who killed him, and partly because I want to know."

"Make you feel better?"

"I don't like it that whoever did this thinks life's so cheap. Someone's life ends so that some kind of point can be made to Trevini. It sucks."

I was getting tense. I wanted more beer but I was driving. I suppose one more couldn't hurt?

"When do you reckon the club will be open again?"

"Daytime? Don't know. But Thursday night, for sure."

"Cool. Then we can get back to stakeout."

"What do you mean *we*, white man?" I asked incredulously.

"You and me. The A-team. Best of the Best." He looked a little hurt.

"Look, thanks for your help already but this shit is getting heavy."

"Hey, no worries. My middle name is heavy."

That made me snort my pint.

"Kelp. Your middle name is Clarence."

We both had to laugh because it actually was. Kelvin Clarence Prentice. When I met him he was calling himself Kel P. Like some bad-ass hip hop B-boy. I told him that Kelpie sounded like a swamp creature of Irish myth and legend. So it became Kelp.

Anyway, I didn't labour the point. I just told him to steer clear of the club until all this was over.

We stacked some coins on the side of the pool table and waited for the current game to finish. There was an offer of 'winner stays on' but we weren't interested.

Kelp played a good game. Managed not to break any windows or rip the baize. Whilst we played he said, "My sister came up last night. When you gonna come meet her?"

I told him I was busy.

When I got home that afternoon there was something

bugging me. Something I was missing. Spreading rumours about drugs was someone's way of having a pop at Club Zed and, by association, Trevini. I was pretty sure now that they were just that. Rumours. I wasn't going to bother trying to trace them to source. Hints would have been dropped around the nightclub scene in general. It was the other clubs that would buy into it, who would want to believe. It would be like trying to grasp the wind. It would be someone's brother's uncle's cousin's sister's friend knew somebody, who heard something.

Forget the drugs. The campaign had been stepped up. The press would run articles: 'Bradford's Battered Body - Ban these Brutal Bouncers' or some such shite.

So why couldn't I forget the drugs? There was something churning away below conscious level. I resolved to have a go at retrieving it. After I'd had a bath.

Paul Britton might call it Unassisted Cognitive Interviewing. Paul McKenna might call it Self-Hypnosis. Jose Silva might call it Alpha Picturing. I don't think any of them would advise that you practise it whilst a cat is sitting on your chest but then I've been told I've something of the maverick in me.

I visualised myself back in the police van. Trying to re-experience as many sights, sounds, smells, whatever. I'd already been plagued by images of the body but now forced myself to pay attention.

He was in his early twenties. His clothes looked absolutely pristine apart from the blood and the rain. They didn't appear to suit him. It was as if they'd been bought the same day - by someone else. His hair was not particularly neat, untypical of a lad dressed that way for a night out. He had an unhealthy look about him but then, hey, he was dead.

I tried to relax even more, not to force any of the images or impressions that were flowing by. Then I heard someone say "Track marks" and I knew what had been bugging me.

I counted up from one to five, opened my eyes and sat up.

The cat made a 'brrrp' noise and ran off downstairs.

Was I just making it all up? False Memory Syndrome's a bugger.

I waited until around 10 p.m, phoned the nick and asked for DS Hadley regarding the investigation at the club. Seeing as he'd been around on Friday I thought he might be doing weekend nights. I was right.

"Hadley..." he answered.

"Hi Phil, got an ID on that dead junkie yet?"

"Who is this?"

So much for subterfuge.

"If I tell you, I'll have to kill you."

"O'Brien." He didn't sound happy.

There was a long pause during which I thought he might just hang up.

"Yes. We do have an ID on 'that dead junkie', as you so sensitively put it, but I'm telling you nothing."

Then he hung up.

Well. He'd told me nothing but he'd kind of confirmed my suspicions by default. A devious bunch we private eyes.

For the guy's name I'd have to wait for the press. Late Monday, early Tuesday I reckoned.

I slept uncomfortably. I've never had a policeman accuse me of insensitivity before.

Chapter 8

Monday. The silicone chip inside my head was switched to overload. I'd done nothing strenuous last night between having a bath and going to bed but I felt distinctly unclean when I awoke.

I took a long shower. The Minging Detective.

I hit the gym early and was soon a sweaty article once again. I finished up and found to my delight that the shower had been fixed over the weekend. I had my second one of the day. All before half ten in the morning.

I phoned Tim and arranged an early lunch over which we made a list of times and dates in the 'let's fuck with Trevini' campaign. Nothing remarkable. There were four letters to four different Northern papers. They appeared to have been written by a well educated person. They were all worded differently and referred to separate alleged incidents. But, taken as a *gestalt*, I'd swear they were of the same hand. Tim looked as tired as he had on Saturday morning and touched hardly any of his Nachos.

I really had nothing else to do for the rest of the afternoon so I put my bike in the back of the car and drove up to Gisburn Forest for a bit of a burn round. It was raining again but when you've got a Cannondale Jekyll that costs more than some people's used cars, you're going to make an effort.

I got home. Flecks of mud all over me had dried on the way back. Third shower of the day. No cat food. No coffee. Off to the shops.

I picked up an evening *Telegraph*. It was in there. Quite subdued and circumspect for the press. I think that they must have got an inkling that there was perhaps more to this than the police were letting on, so they didn't want to play a strong editorial hand as yet.

There was a brief quote from Trevini saying how terrible

this was. The article said a reward was being offered for any information leading to the capture of those responsible. It gave my mobile number. That had been my idea and he had gone for it. Wasn't going to ingratiate us with the police, though.

The dead guy was called Mark Fawcett and had been from Salford, Greater Manchester. Nothing about him being a drug user, but then that's not the kind of thing that would have been relevant to the press at this stage. Probably not that relevant to the police either.

It was the only lead I had though, so I was sure as hell going to make it relevant.

I felt like Mark's drug use may have made him an easy target for someone's manipulation. I felt like it may have contributed to the opinion of whoever killed him that it was okay to do so. He was 'just a junkie'. You're going to kill someone so you dehumanise them first. You make them less important than you.

Drug dependency is often linked to low self esteem. Drugs help you escape the shittiness of who you are. For a while at least. Most people who become dependent on drugs then end up hating themselves for doing so. Most of them, at some point, seek some form of help - even if they have no faith in it themselves, they might do it to please someone who matters to them, they might do it to make the courts more lenient.

One of the most popular forms of help are voluntary organisations which provide non-judgmental advice and support. They sometimes provide clean needles - if you aren't going to stop people using then at least reduce the potential harm via safer usage.

I wondered if Mark Fawcett had ever used such a service.

I did an internet search. The closest drug advisory service to the Salford area was called the 'Bacchus Project'. Cool name. I would ring them in the morning.

I spoke to my granddad on the phone about prostate

glands and Voltarol and then watched *L.A. Confidential* for about the 300th time before going to bed.

Tuesday. I phoned and spoke to a girl called Abby Marchant. I tried to establish as much rapport as I could, asking about the service they provided. I thought about throwing in a remark like "have you seen Mark lately?" to catch her off guard. But if they did know him then maybe they'd heard about his demise as well, so I didn't want to make her feel awkward.

I still felt guilty for what I'd said to Hadley. I played it as straight as I could.

"Look, I don't quite know how to say this, but I have reason to believe that you may have worked with someone named Mark Fawcett..."

Abby butted in.

"Such information is strictly confidential." Defensive. Professional.

"Please hear me out. If you do know Mark Fawcett, and you haven't already heard, then I'm very sorry to tell you that he died last Friday night. He was killed. I'm investigating his death and I'd really appreciate any help that you can give me."

Silence.

"Check that what I'm saying is true if you wish. Are you online over there?" I gave her the phone number of the *Telegraph* but also the website address so that she could read the article.

"Please ring me back if you can offer any help at all." I gave her my mobile number. I told her that if she read the article she would see it was the same number given in that.

She mumbled something that sounded like she was agreeing and hung up.

It was forty minutes before she phoned back. I had a false start, though, about ten minutes into the wait when my mobile rang. Just before picking up I saw that a Bradford number was coming up on the screen.

"O'Brien."

"I'm phoning about that reward, yeah?" The voice was male, white and I would hazard a guess at ill-educated. I had it down straight away as a piss-take but you can never be sure.

"Do you have some information?"

"Yeah, I saw that bloke getting paggered. It were some Paki lads."

"Some?"

"Yeah." Hesitation. "Five of 'em. Fucking cowards eh?"

"Is that why you didn't intervene? Too many of them?"

"I chased 'em off, didn't I?"

"Of course you did. Can you recall what any of them were wearing?"

"I don't know? Fucking pajamas, like they do." You could hear his mate in the background laughing at that.

"Okay. What's your address?"

"Are you going to bring the reward?"

Do you know, he sounded like he really believed I would.

"No. I'm going to come round and put my foot in your arse."

He hung up and I left it at that. I could keep the number in my phone and find out the address if I really wanted to, if I ever got bored.

I filled the rest of the time by practising the *Sil Lim Tao* Wing Chun form, but real slow so I didn't get all sweaty. The phone rang just as I finished off and did a little *shaolin* bow to no one in particular.

"Are you the police?" she asked straight off.

"No. I'm a private investigator, hired by the owner of the club outside which Mark was found. I'm also the person who found his body."

"Perhaps I should be talking to the police..."

"Miss Marchant, I very much doubt that the police will be contacting you. They've identified Mark but I don't think they'll be interested in 'who he was', if you know what I mean."

"And you are?"

"Yes. I want to know about him. I want to find some meaning in his death. If I understand why he died it might help me to understand who is responsible."

"Might?"

"It's the way I work."

Silence again.

"You sound upset." Me in counselling mode.

"I am." She paused. "I knew Mark well." She said it very quietly.

"Then please help me. It won't be a betrayal. I'm not going to ask you to tell me anything you don't feel comfortable with."

She took a deep breath and collected herself.

"Okay."

"Can we meet this lunchtime?"

"Erm, it would have to be after two o'clock."

"What if we meet at Victoria, two-thirty, round about where the WH Smith's stand is?"

"Yes. How will I recognise you?"

I looked down at myself. I was wearing blue Levi's and a black Diesel T-shirt with the tiniest of logos.

"I look like Johnny Bravo but with bigger legs."

"Who?"

"Don't worry. I'll find you."

"And how will you recognise me?" She said it with forced patience but amusement, like talking to a child.

"Miss Marchant, I *am* a detective."

She gave a quiet laugh and I was glad to hear it for her sake.

I took the train. It's a pleasant journey. On the way you can even see my mum's house in Hebden Bridge. Once you get there you can *easy* take the Metro to the shops and stuff. It's very hip, very cosmopolitan. All in all, Manchester looks and feels a lot better since the IRA decided to bomb it. There's

51

also nothing quite like the feeling of finding a 'lead' and I was in a relatively good mood.

There were plenty of people who looked like they were waiting for someone but Abby Marchant was the only one who looked like she was waiting for a detective.

I guessed her at early twenties. She looked like a drug worker. Then again, so do most of Manchester. She was about five-foot-five and dressed head to toe in Gothic black. She had a nose stud, little John Lennon specs and her long raven black hair was pulled back tight. She was maybe three stone overweight but it suited her. I wondered if she was glad I hadn't asked her to describe herself.

"Hi, I'm Johnny Bravo," I said as I approached.

"Where's the shades?"

"I thought you didn't know?"

"I phoned a friend."

We both chuckled. Abby Marchant and I were going to get along just dandy.

On the Metro we made small talk. I told her I liked Manchester. She said she did too, she'd moved from York to study there, had got into drugs, had got out of them again, and had ended up with this job. She'd lightened up even more since the phone call. I figure that if you're a drug worker you might have to get used to the occasional death of a client. Mark must have been a likeable guy for her to be doing this.

We got off as near to the Village as the tram lines will take you, skirted the edge of Chinatown, and walked to Via Fossa for drinks. It's a very roomy place but in a cosy kind of way. At that time of day it was easy to find a dark and quite spot, up on the balcony, where we could talk in private.

To those of you not in the know, Via Fossa is a gay bar. One of many in the Village but definitely the best. Recommend it. If you go in the summer, then ask for a plastic glass and take it out front onto the cobbles, breathe in the heady organic, aromatic mixture of lager, Joop! and stagnant canal water, then smile as you watch the most beautiful assortment of people parade past, proud as peacocks. As fearless as any tough guy would aspire to.

"Are you gay then?" asked Abby as I bought the beers over. Both pint drinkers.

"Such information is strictly confidential," I countered.

"Sure," she said.

I'm not as it happens. But perhaps I should experiment with the ambiguous pop star chic. Maybe I'd get more work that way. Chris O'Brien - The Gay Detective. It had a ring to it. *He's here, he's queer, he's without peer and if you're buyin' he's drinkin beer.*

She opened a baccy tin and took out a roll-up that she must have prepared earlier.

I basically let her speak. She told me about Mark Fawcett as a person. He'd been a popular person at the project. He was a good car mechanic by all accounts but couldn't hold down a regular job. That sort of thing. She sighed frequently. After a while she said,

"Is any of this helping?"

"Maybe. Sounds like Mark was a friendly guy. What I think is that someone befriended him, probably with a little bit of brown as leverage, maybe got him doing errands, odd jobs, whatever. Gained his confidence. Then killed him."

"Why?"

"This is what I'd call an 'organised' killing. It has a goal, an intended outcome. Killing Mark wasn't the goal. He's just a means to an end. Of course, he could have just been snatched off the streets but I don't think so. Too risky, too disorganised. I think Mark would have been 'seduced' and I think being a user made that all the easier for someone to do."

"Is this what they call 'profiling'?"

"It's guesswork. Which I suppose is what profiling amounts to..."

"I still can't see how any of this helps."

53

"It may not. But if that's close to what happened then maybe he'll have spoken to someone, said 'hey, I've made this great new friend' that kind of..."

She gripped my arm.

"Oh my God! You're right! When I last saw him he said he'd met these two lads from down south, raved about them. He said they were helping him out, were going to get him some work!"

"Okay, calm down Abby. It may be totally unrelated. Did he describe these lads?"

"Not really. It wasn't what I was interested in at the time."

She sounded like she felt guilty. I told her it was okay.

"Where down south were they from?"

"Er, not London. Somewhere rural. I know that because of the kind of work he was talking about. He was going to go down there and do some sort of farm work, fixing tractors and things. I'm sorry I can't be more specific."

I told her it was okay again.

She told me she'd last seen him a week ago yesterday and that was when he'd told her about these lads. She didn't keep a home address on him and probably wouldn't have felt comfortable giving it to me if she did. She knew he'd mentioned that he lived with his mum, on and off, and that her name was Anna.

I asked her how she felt. She said she felt better for talking and she hoped she had helped me. I said she had been very helpful. She asked me how I felt. It catches me off guard when people do that.

"I feel angry, Abby. Now I know more about Mark it makes me angry that he was used like this."

I thought about the way he'd been dressed. Had they tricked him into that clubber's outfit before killing him? Had they struggled with him? At what horrific point did it dawn on him that his 'friends' were really his captors?

"So you're going to 'avenge' Mark's death?"

The Gay Avenger - that sounded even better.

"Yeah, I am. And defend my employer's honour into the bargain."

She shook her head, But I could tell she was impressed just the same.

I finished my pint. My mouth was dry from gobbing off. I asked if she wanted to go for lunch. On expenses. She said she never ate during the day. I raised my eyebrows but didn't make any wisecracks.

I said she could call me any time and gave her a card. It was the one that said: *Gangstas & villains u know they b dyin' if they b messin' wiv Chris O'Brien.*

"Hmm, classy," she said doubtfully.

So I gave her another one. It was this season's Haiku:

Autumn leaves fall fast
O'Brien searches for clues
Penetrates like wind

She appeared to like that one better.

I offered to accompany her back to work but she had an appointment elsewhere. We said our goodbyes and I got a bus into Salford. Whilst sitting on the bus my mobile vibrated. It was a text message from Abby. It said: *"To catch a killer, he's going to try, Chris O'Brien - Catcher in the Rye."*

Chapter 9

It took me longer than I thought to find Salford town hall. Town halls tend to be conspicuously grand in their design and fairly centrally placed so I got off the bus in what I took to be the centre of town. A couple of discreet enquiries of passers-by put me on the bus again heading back out of Salford on Swinton Road. So much for my skills of detection.

The building was a twentieth century monstrosity. Now called the Civic Centre. I asked a man at a desk, in a hallway that I considered too brightly lit, if I could look through the electoral register. He asked if I had an appointment. I said no, did I need one? He said no I didn't need one and yes I could. I ask you?

Salford had twenty electoral wards. Big. There were eleven Fawcetts in all. Not too bad. There was only one Fawcett, Annabel. Registered at the same house were a Fawcett, Mark and a Fawcett, Barry. The address was Pendleton, which meant I could attempt to visit on my way back into town, although I was wishing now I had brought the car.

I travelled back, found the house, braced myself, and knocked at the door.

The woman who answered was in her mid-forties and had the look of the recently bereaved. Tired, red-eyed, bewildered.

"Mrs. Fawcett?" I said with as much compassion as you can cram into so small a question.

"Are you from...Victim Support?" She said it hesitantly, as if she wasn't sure she had the words correct and then half-sighed, the sound sticking in her throat, strangling and almost obliterating what she said next: "You'd better come in," she croaked.

There was no way I was going to deceive her on that count.

"No Mrs. Fawcett, I'm not. I'm very sorry..."

She stopped me mid flow.

"You'd better come in," she repeated with more force this time. Her hand motioned for me to do as she said. Her face scanned up and down the street, wearing a hunted look.

I did as she said. She seemed anxious just to get me off the doorstep, and in was the quickest way. I could understand why. The sense of twitching curtains, fuelled by the lingering public spectacle of recent visitors to the house. It was palpable.

"Neighbours not making things any easier?" I said. She didn't say anything.

I took a seat. Sometimes it's more polite just to do that than wait for someone to play the etiquette game and offer you one. She had enough on her mind. On a large pine coffee table were some leaflets that had probably been left there by the police. Victim Support was one. A bereavement counselling service was another.

When she took a seat I told her who I was and offered condolences on behalf of myself and the club. Formality. That might be all she was ready to deal with right now. I left it hanging at the bit about being a representative of the club. She might want to blame us. I tried to convey without speaking that, if that's how she felt and that's what she wanted to do, then that was what I was there for and that it was okay. That's a lot to convey, but they say the human face can be very expressive.

She told me that she didn't blame the club. See?

Anna went on to say that the police had told her that Mark had probably sustained his injuries elsewhere and that none of the door staff were under suspicion. She said it all seemed very odd and I agreed with her.

She was sitting on the edge of her seat, leaning forward, wringing her hands. She had made only fleeting eye contact since my arrival. She seemed so far away, so alone.

I leaned forward in my seat, took a deep breath, let it out, and spoke.

"Anna, these last few days must have been awful for you. How are you coping?"

She looked at me properly for the first time. I tried to imagine myself oozing compassion and supportiveness from every pore. I have quite an imagination. She looked back at her hands.

"I don't even know." She sighed.

"No one could expect you to. It must feel unreal."

"Yes it does. It's all been..."

She was lost for words and sort of waved her hand briefly in front of her face at eye level.

"A blur?"

She nodded and continued.

"The police. The questions. Not knowing where to put myself or what to say."

"Feeling out of place and confused, but having to deal with it just the same," I offered.

"Yes. I've had to contact Barry, Mother, my sister. No one knows what to say."

"It sounds like you are trying really hard."

"I've got to be strong,..."

She said it doubtfully as if it was something that someone had once told her she had to be and that now maybe she no longer believed it, or was scared that she would let them down.

"Anna. No one can tell you how you are supposed to feel right now. However you feel is...okay. It's allowed."

Her shoulders started to shake, the rest of her body began to follow. I went to her and held her. It was the right thing to do. She held me in return, buried her face into my chest, and sobbed.

We stayed like that for quite some time until first her shaking, then her sobbing began to subside. Eventually she spoke, very softly, face still pressed against me.

"I feel so...alone."

I nodded slowly, so she could feel the movement. We

gently released each other. She looked at me. Her eyes, though red and moist with tears, seemed clearer. It was as if by speaking her feelings out loud she had firmed her grip on the world, had reconnected with reality.

"It's okay to feel that way. It's okay," I said.

Anna Fawcett began to talk. It was as if she'd been waiting for permission to do so all her life.

She told me it had been a few weeks since she had seen Mark. They generally got on when they did see each other but he tended to stay away a lot - 'ashamed' of his drug use. She wished he hadn't felt like that, she would just have preferred to see more of him. There was only one occasion when he had stolen from her. He had stayed away for ages after that. Barry was his brother, younger by a year. They shared a bedroom in the small house. He was off with the army in Catterick and had said he hoped he could get home by tomorrow on compassionate leave. There was no Mr. Fawcett, not for the last fourteen years anyway. She had escaped his violence and said she'd not had much luck with men since. Said that you couldn't trust them, could you? Then she looked embarrassed, she'd forgotten I was one. It happens. I gave her the universe's most pathetic smile.

She asked if I wanted to see Mark and Barry's bedroom. It was what the police had done. I thanked her. I didn't think I'd find anything useful but I didn't want to decline the kindness of her offer.

The room was sparse and neat. Probably Barry's army influence. There was a large Blues Brothers poster on one wall. Quite a collection of fantasy novels along a shelf. Stephen Donaldson and David Eddings. I wondered idly which brother they belonged to. If I was looking for a missing person then a search of their personal effects might provide more clues. I couldn't imagine that he would have left any sort of clues that would lead to his killers.

If Mark Fawcett had been a 15-year-old girl then maybe there'd be a diary - "met these two boys, Simon and Adrian, I think they like me. I like Simon best, he's got his own tractor," - that sort of thing - maybe some passport size snapshots of the three of them goofing off in a photo booth. But no.

The timeframe was probably wrong anyway. From what Abby, then Anna, had told me, Mark was very unlikely to have spoken to his mother about his new found 'chums'. I headed back downstairs and resolved not even to ask her directly.

She had made me a cup of tea. We sat and talked for a while longer, I asked if she knew any of Mark's friends. She snorted and said not since he was around twelve.

I asked her how she was feeling now and she said much better - then caught herself, the guilt of the bereaved. She looked at me like she wanted me to tell her it was okay to feel better.

I did. I told her that it sounded like she had been dealing with the loss of Mark for quite some time before he died. She nodded. I said she'd probably gone through stages of denial, anger, bargaining and depression, as if Mark had been terminally ill. She could identify with that too.

We both paused. Both knowing that it wasn't enough.

Mark hadn't died of an overdose, or AIDS, or malnutrition. Someone had killed him. Somebody had decided that his life was going to end.

"Anna," I said quietly but firmly, "I'm going to find who killed your son."

If you don't make promises like that too often, and if you really mean them when you do, then the *Dao* will carry you through. I believe that.

It was the kind of promise I could never have made as a nurse. That's partly why I left.

She looked into my eyes.

"Thank you," she said.

I told her she could talk to me anytime and gave her a card. A straight one.

Chapter 10

Wednesday. When I'd got home last night I hadn't felt hungry so I just sat and drank beer to beat the band. Consequently the morning found me knocking back a litre of water before forcing myself out the door to run a figure-of-eight route that took me up two unforgiving climbs and through more mud and dead leaf mulch than I would have liked. It took me through Heaton woods and across the golf course that commands a view of Bingley, Shipley and some of the taller landmarks of Bradford – like Lister's mill chimney, resplendent in its baroque Italian glory. You might think the city's just traffic jams and urban decay from what I've been telling you, but the route I was running was only a ten minute walk from where the Manningham riots took place in '96, and there are still deer in those woods. Two different worlds - minutes apart. I love that. You can lie in the grass and listen to the drumming of a busy woodpecker. No traffic noise. You could be anywhere. But if City are playing, and if they score, then you can hear the cheer go up from Valley Parade, over two miles away. Rural and urban merge and complement each other. It's a Yin Yang thing.

The run didn't kill me, so it must have made me stronger. Afterwards I felt better for it.

Following a breakfast of cornmeal pancakes and an apple sliced and fried in butter I decided I would return to Salford for the day. There might be some scope in trying to find and talk to other people who had known Mark. I phoned the Bacchus Project and asked for Abby. She seemed pleased to hear from me. I told her about my afternoon with Mrs. Fawcett and she said she wished she could meet and talk with her. I told her Anna might appreciate that too. Then I revealed my plan of walking the streets of Salford hassling the local users and dealers. She told me some potentially useful places to go and a couple of possibly relevant names. She told me to pop into the Project for a cuppa and I said I would.

"Chris, you be careful out there. Guns are not unheard of, you know."

"Have faith, Miss Marchant. I've spent a large part of my morning leaping tall buildings with a single bound. I am equal to the task."

"Hmm. If you say so. See you later. I hope." She hung up.

Hmm indeed. The young lady was trying to sound unimpressed - and failing miserably I might add.

I took the train again. If you're going to walk the mean streets then you might as well go for it and really walk. Besides, if I got rolled then I wasn't going to lose anything but the cash I was carrying. The cash was there to ease the flow of information if I managed to get anyone talking. I'd gone and got a hundred quid's worth of fivers from the bank. Thoughtfully, I had then changed a couple of them down into pound coins - I figured that if O'Brien was going to spend another day righting wrongs in the big city, then the homeless should know about it too.

I found my way to an attempt at a pedestrianised shopping area in Eccles that I really hoped had once seen better days. Most of the shop fronts were closed down and boarded up, many with heavy roll-down metal shutters. There was a newsagents, a bookie's and a pharmacy still doing business but from behind thick mesh and toughened glass. The newsagents displayed a sign saying that it sold 'Fancy Goods'. Fancy that. I went in and bought ten cigs and a lighter. It would give me something to do with my hands whilst I was skulking and it might make me look more the part. No, scrub that. I've already told you about me and smoking.

I sat on a low wall for a bit and then skulked over and sat on a bench for a bit too. I was looking kind of obvious but that was part of the plan. Eventually, a geezer in an oversize Kickers jacket came over and offered me his wares.

"Naa, cheers mate. I'm sorted. Waiting for someone. You know Mark?"

He blanked me and strolled away to pastures new. Charming. Last time I score off him.

People came and went. I shared my cigs with some girls who probably should have been in school and gave them some chat. At one point a guy approached me and asked if I was selling. I felt like I had arrived big style.

Then I saw Woody. I knew it was Woody because Abby had told me to look out for the Jewish skinhead and there he was so. Shaved head and a strong nose. His baggy white Kappa shell suit did nothing for his painfully thin physique and pale skin. I waited until he had gone into the betting shop and come out again. Then I collared him.

"You Woody?"

"Yeah..." You could tell he had wanted to say 'who wants to know' but had probably been slapped in the past for doing so and now knew better.

"You know Mark Fawcett." A statement not a question. "Have you seen him around?"

"Not recently, mate."

"Can we have a chat?"

He seemed not to know whether it would be safe to refuse. If only he knew the compassionate me. We sat on the bench that I'd been hogging earlier. I told him Mark was missing. He didn't react like he'd heard anything to the contrary. I told him that his mum was worried and that I was a friend of Abby Marchant. He nodded when I said that. I asked when he'd last seen Mark and he said it had been about two weeks ago. I peeled off four of my notes and handed him two. The way he made them disappear warranted a round of applause and honorary membership of the Magic Circle. I said I was interested in anything he could tell me about Mark's behaviour the last few times he had seen him and that if I was impressed then a further tenner would change hands.

Woody did his best to please. Mark had been really buzzing the last couple of times he saw him, handing out various goodies to people he knew. Woody explained a little bit about how their local scene worked in that a bunch of people dealt to each other depending on their circumstances at any given time. The supply, however, was from one source only. You could buy from whoever you wished, because maybe you'd fallen out with someone, or you owed them something and didn't have enough to pay back but had just enough to score from someone else. You could sort all that shit out between you but if you were interested in supplying then you could only go to one person.

I listened with interest. It was like a lecture on feudalism or trade agreements.

Then he told me that Mark had gone outside of source. That was even more interesting.

Mark was aware of his folly but didn't seem to care. He said his new suppliers were his 'mates' and he would be going away soon anyway. He hadn't asked where. Woody told me that word had got back to the local supplier and he had paid Mark a visit. Shit. So maybe no one was surprised he had 'disappeared.'

Woody seemed reluctant to speak a name. I sighed and absent mindedly rubbed the notes back and forth between my fingers. Woody shrugged and said the name 'Javeed Ali'. I guess he sensed my tenacity.

I gave him fifteen quid. I'm a hell of a guy.

Around lunchtime I called into the Project. Me and Abby had a brew and I donated any unsmoked cigs that I had left. I told her about my morning and asked her about Javeed. He was the 'Mr. Big' of the immediate area, although she also explained that this didn't have to mean he was particularly high up in the whole Manchester hierarchy. She also pointed out that it wasn't their job to gather 'intelligence'. None of the workers had ever knowingly met Javeed but one of his guys, Nassir, was a local face. Apparently you couldn't miss him. She gave a description and I saw why. She had no suggestions as to where to look for him, though.

We said our goodbyes and she gave me another warning. Yeah yeah.

I decided I was just going to wander round asking people "Where's Javeed?". Annoy people and see what happens. I can do annoying.

It worked. A couple of hours later I was dry-mouthed, foot-sore and another ten quid lighter. I was coming out of cafe popping open a can a Pepsi Max when a black BMW 3 Series pulled up. Alloys, tinted windows - the full gangsta option pack. Nassir, for it was he, got out of the back and held the door open for me.

"Get in," said the Asian man-mountain.

He didn't pat me down, and even let me hang on to my Pepsi. He got in after me and the car didn't creak when he sat. Good suspension on these babies. The driver looked way too young with his bum-fluff moustache and I nearly asked him what he'd thought of the written test. I thought better of it, like I was in a 'speak when you're spoken to' situation. We all remained silent but nodded along to Tupac. It all felt pretty relaxed. Relatively speaking.

The building we arrived at was some sort of renovated mill. Fairly squat. Two or three storeys at most. I got the impression it backed onto a canal but I couldn't be sure. I ditched my empty can before entering. Nassir accompanied me through the doors and up the stairs, making me go first. We went through two different heavy duty dead-bolted doors and I noticed a state-of the-art alarm system too.

We entered the 'room' that was basically, save the stairwell, one whole floor of the building.

There was Javeed.

The first thing I noticed about him was the gun.

I'm no firearms expert but I watch a lot of telly. It was a Beretta. An Italian handgun favoured by the military. Capable of firing thirteen bullets before having to reload. It was nickel plated. It looked cool, clipped to his belt like that. I was glad he wasn't pointing it at me. That would not have looked cool.

Javeed's suit was also of Italian design. Perhaps he was trying to take over Trevini's restaurants. As a style thing.

Apart from him, the rest of the place was Asian chic. No comment. A hideous cream coloured carpet covered most of the room. It was obviously expensive but still tacky. I bet there were some grand floorboards underneath, just begging to be sanded and varnished. There were two great big leather sofas. Possibly Italian too but they didn't go with the carpet. There was a glass coffee table! Like you expected the cast of *Miami Vice* to turn up and start snorting coke off it. The blinds on the numerous windows were pulled down and were all adorned with a star of Pakistan logo. A plethora of strip lighting hung from the ceiling. Panoramic photographs in large clip frames hung from the wall. They were all of Karachi mountain territory, from different viewpoints, each with a Mosque dotted somewhere within the scenery.

At the far end of the room I could see through a bamboo partition that there was a heavy bag and a speed ball suspended from the ceiling. On the wall there was a poster of 'Prince' Naseem Hamed. From that distance I couldn't swear to it but I think it was signed. No carpet up there but it appeared to be lino. Lino? Give me strength.

"Have you searched our guest, Nassir?" spoke Javeed. His eyes not leaving me.

My driving companion shrugged. Like it didn't matter whether he had or hadn't. Then he did so anyway. I suppose to keep his boss happy. A boss is a boss but a boss with a gun, well, what can you say?

Nassir was big. Maybe six-three and 300lbs. Still fit into Large Benny's pocket though. His hands moved deftly over me. He left me with my loose change and lighter but chucked my wad over to Javeed, who caught it just as deftly.

"He's clean, boss," Nassir pronounced, before shifting his bulk over to one of the sofas and collapsing onto it. The sofa hissed in protest but didn't collapse.

"Well, what have you to say, my friend?" Javeed to me.

"*Ass-a-laam-oo-alaikum,*" I said.

"*Alaikum-salaam,*" he replied almost automatically, caught himself, then smiled.

"Well, well," said Nassir, nodding to himself. I sensed approval. I like approval.

"I apologise for the formalities." Javeed waved his hand in a dismissive gesture. "May I offer you a drink?"

"No thank you. It would be impolite of me. You guys must have, what..." I looked at my watch for effect, "another two hours to go?"

The month of Ramadan had started the day before yesterday and if these two were good Muslims, drug dealing aside, then no food or drink would be passing their lips from sun up to sun down. Maybe they were taking sustenance intravenously - never thought of that.

I hoped that Nassir was glad at not having to leave his seat and play butler too. Might approve of me even more.

"Yes. Indeed." Javeed sounded solemn, even a little bit embarrassed.

"They tell me it gets easier after the first couple of days."

"You have Muslim friends?"

"One or two. I'm from Bradford."

They both nodded. Thankfully they didn't launch into that 'Oh, do you know so-and-so?' routine. We got down to business.

I told them I was a private investigator working *pro bono* as a friend of Mark Fawcett's family. I lied and said Mark was missing. I half lied and said they were not under suspicion as far as I was concerned. I said truthfully that I was interested in finding out who Mark's new suppliers had been.

Javeed was very helpful. He seemed quite proprietorial towards his 'flock'. He said that Nassir had spoken to Mark and, whilst the threat of violence had been implicit, none had been necessary. Mark had apologised and said his suppliers had no intention of cutting in on the local scene. They were mates from down south and he would be moving down there himself. I asked if he had been any more precise than just down south. Javeed looked at Nassir, who then said, "Dorset."

Ah, the rural lads. Funny that. I know Dorset fairly well as it happens.

Then Javeed asked me who had mentioned his name. I smiled enigmatically and said some stuff about client confidentiality.

Nassir smiled predatorily and said some stuff about breaking my legs.

I had lost a bit of faith in Nassir and was thinking he couldn't be all that as a minder. I had managed to sidle up to within groin kicking distance of his boss and he hadn't moved a muscle. I could slam Javeed in the family jewels and take that gun away from him.

Never done owt like that. I do watch *a lot* of telly though.

The scene had been set for a bit of showing off and, to be honest, I think we were all enjoying the theatricality of it. People meet a real life PI and they think they're in a movie. I even had to remind myself it was real sometimes.

"What if I decide to keep this, my friend?" Javeed waved my wad in the air.

"Then, my friend, we get to see how quick on the draw you are." I spread my hands.

They both laughed then. That cleared the tension. I figured sixty-odd quid wouldn't cover the clean-up cost if he did cap me. Life may be cheap but carpeting is anything but.

"Javeed, Nassir. This has been helpful to me and I thank you for your time. You are welcome to take from my money whatever you feel your time is worth." Polite. Respectful.

He tossed the money over to me.

"It is of no consequence." No consequence. That Javeed. Drama queen. "But whilst you are here, is there perhaps anything we can supply for you?"

I made a thoughtful face.

"Got any of those bath salts for tired feet?"

That cracked them up. I'll take my approval from anywhere. I nearly asked them if they could sort me for fresh dhania, but even I have boundaries I won't cross. They wished me well as I was leaving, we shook hands and I told them "*Shuk-ria*" and "*Khuda-hafaze.*" It was difficult not to warm to them. Drug dealers are people too.

Yet as I walked away, reorienting myself to whichever part of Manchester I was now in, an unwanted image invaded my mind. As if it had seeped into my skull from the heavy air around me. I was back in the dark wet alley behind the club. Shining a torch down on Mark's lifeless, battered body. Only this time Anna was there too, kneeling over him, shaking and sobbing like before. I wanted to hold her. I wanted to tell her it was okay. But I couldn't move a muscle nor utter a sound.

A shaft of sunlight, perhaps the last of the day, shone from behind a dense pink-edged cloud low on the western skyline and the image faded as quickly as it came.

So much for friendly drug dealers. A pin had been stuck in my warmth balloon.

A couple of streets later I leaned over a hedge and threw up.

I think it was the gun.

Chapter 11

Thursday. But only barely just. I was woken by my mobile, snatching it up from the bedside table with an adrenaline jolt. Backlit in green, it told me the time was 3.17 am. Caller ID told me it was Tim Marconi, which did nothing to quell my adrenaline levels, I can tell you.

"O'Brien Investigations - we never sleep."

I have this theory that taking the piss helps to combat stress.

"You're the one who's always telling people to call anytime."

This is true.

"Listen Chris, there's been a fire."

That got me sitting bolt upright, giving the cat an adrenaline rush too where the mobile had failed. The cat's blasé when it comes to noises but it can't stand sudden movements. It tore off from under the duvet.

Tim continued.

"Over at Unit 5. It's out now. Security guard handled it but he's pretty shaken. Fire brigade are over there now. I'm on my way."

"Me too. See you there." I pulled on the tracksuit and Reeboks that were still on the floor from yesterday morning's run. Dried mud and all.

Unit 5 was the last in a row of five externally identical box-like one storey buildings that sat alongside the local railway line. Not exactly an industrial estate but you get the idea.

Trevini has a small wine importing business. He supplies all his own clubs and restaurants and a good few other places besides. This was the delivery warehouse and the office that dealt with the business side of it. No one had had the imagination to call the place anything different. The building next door housed a small laser art company called 'Unit 4 Printing'. Apathy.

As I approached the locale I began cruising quietly around the nearby streets. If this had been arson - and I can't see Tim calling me otherwise - then maybe the culprit was still around. They do that. Admire their handiwork from a nearby vantage point, quite possibly wanking off to the sound of sirens. I scanned the rooftops, doorways, fire escapes and eyeballed the nearby railway bridge. Nada. I tried to make a mental note of any vehicles that were around in case I saw them again in suspicious circumstances. I was getting too into it, had the entire surrounding area mapped out in mnemonics. Finally, I stopped trying to be clever and pulled in behind Tim's parked car.

A fire engine was still there. Also an unmarked Vectra that gave itself away as Old Bill due to its lack of parking finesse.

I nodded at Tim and Dean, the young security guard, as I passed. I would catch up with them in a bit but it looked as if the brigade were packing up and I wanted to speak to them. I walked up to the only one who wasn't clambering back into the truck. He was talking to two CID guys. I attempted to convey the impression I owned the place.

"I came as soon as I heard. Terrible business. What can you tell me?"

The three of them eyed me suspiciously. Perhaps I should have worn a suit.

The fireman drew breath.

"Same as I've been telling everyone else. Arson. Accelerant poured under that metal shutter - also squirted into the lock and round the frame of your back door there." He pointed to the places he was talking about.

When he had said the word 'squirted' one of the coppers held up a washing up liquid bottle in a sealed transparent plastic bag.

"Sloppy work, and your man acted quickly. Minimal damage. I can't see your insurers having a problem with it."

I thanked him for coming and off he went. I turned to the two officers.

"Have you spoken to Dean yet?"

"Your security man? Not as yet. We've just got here ourselves." I took the speaker to be the more senior of the two in his smart Burberry overcoat.

"Do you know any of the run up to this?" I asked.

"There does seem to be some sort of *vendetta* against Mr.Trevini, does there not, Mr. O'Brien?" He sounded pleased with himself either because he'd twigged who I was or maybe because he'd slipped an Italian word into the conversation.

I suggested that we all go inside, get the kettle on, chat, and view the security camera playback together. I was surprised at how amenable the police were being. I think the bit about the kettle swung it.

The police questioned Dean whilst we sat there and listened. The lad had done well. He'd actually heard something going on before the alarm went off, he'd gone to the shutter door at the back and watched the flames whoosh underneath it. Luckily a stone floor, not much to combust. He ran back for the extinguisher and then noticed the wooden door was on fire too when he got there.

We all praised him, police included. He looked to be in shock now. The scary thing was that he could easily have been killed and whoever had started the fire could not care less. Tim ordered him a taxi home and said he'd cover until the day staff came on. Tim looked like shit himself, bags under both eyes and a tic over one of them. He looked like he was either about to fall asleep, or kill someone. I asked Tim about the site manager, getting her to come in early. He said they'd spoken and she had felt there would be no need for her to be there, seeing as he was attending.

It was around 4.15 a.m by then. I phoned her.

"Who is this? Do you know what time it is?"

I answered her two questions then went on to explain the

situation. She would be in directly. There had been some force in my voice but no curse words had been necessary.

"Women," I said, loud enough for everyone to hear, after I hung the phone up. I'm not a sexist. I was saying it to ingratiate myself with the police, who generally are.

"You mentioned a video?" said Burberry. Like we were a bunch of lads home from the pub. The other officer, who was wearing thick glasses, burped his tea. See? Unreconstructed.

We wound it back and watched on the black and white monitor. The camera was positioned to cover most of the back wall of the building and some of the gate area to the yard. A vehicle couldn't come in and no one could go through either door without being recorded. As ever with a fixed camera there was a blind spot. This one was off to the left and maybe about a fifth of the yard wasn't covered.

The footage wasn't that dramatic whilst rewinding. We could see some flames from the wooden door but the camera was angled from above and everything was really blurred. The flames subsided and blinked out in reverse, then we could see a dark figure by the door. Just.

When we stopped the rewind and played it back we could see why it was blurred. There was a shadow of movement from the edge of the blind spot and then something was squirted at the camera lens. Thick and viscous. Most likely diesel.

"Clever bastard!" Both I and the cop with the glasses happened to say it in unison.

You could still see what was going on, but in black and white, with the arsonist in dark clothes and a balaclava, through a film of diesel, it wasn't exactly going to jog any memories on *Crimewatch*.

The dark figure continued squirting fuel onto the door. Another figure, in similar garb, emerged from the blind spot and began pouring from a five litre petrol carrier under the metal shutter door. They ignited pretty much simultaneously and were off.

"Two man team." said Burberry.

No shit, Sherlock, I thought. I wondered whether to pretend I could tell which part of the country they were from by the way they ran but I decided to button it.

You could almost hear Tim grinding the enamel off his teeth. I told him that we would get these guys, for sure. I was making these promises with no idea how I was going to back them up mind.

I could feel the frowns of the policemen behind me as I gave my reassurances to Tim. But they thanked me for the tea and didn't give me the gypsy warning. They took the tape with them.

Julie, the manager, turned up.

"Bad hair day?" I said.

She was not amused.

Tim left but not before we had made a 3.00 p.m appointment with each other for later in the day. Just me and Julie now. I kept at it until I got a smile out of her and then I left too. I cruised the area one last time but the only thing that looked remotely suspicious was me. Off home and back to bed.

The cat stared at me suspiciously from on top of the wardrobe. I stared back and said "What?" But it just blinked and carried right on.

When I got up again, at a more reasonable hour, I typed a report of the investigation to date. It didn't read very well. Jumping about from event to incident. It was difficult to be anything other than reactive at the moment. Yeah, 'reactive' sounds better than 'floundering'.

Then I spent a bit of time on kicking practice and pretending I was taking guns away from people. Then I spent a bit of time looking in the mirror and saying "You talkin' to me?". Then I realised it was time to get some fresh air.

I walked the streets again. It had been that kind of week. Town was on the busy side and the shops were full of

Christmas stuff. Goodwill toward men. Except those A-holes from Dorset, obviously.

Bradford, for whatever reasons, seems to have traditionally been a place people have fled to. It has become home to many migrant populations. The industrial background, I suppose. The largest and most well known group would be the Asians - a group than can be subdivided into Pakistani, Bengali and Indian. What you don't always hear about are the West Indians, Ukrainians, Polish and Irish. A good friend of mine describes the city as being made up of 'peasant stock', which accounts for why there are so many ugly people in Bradford. It's difficult not to agree.

It's a city I've grown to love. Just small enough to feel you know it in its entirety. Just big enough to keep coming up with surprises. I could only ever feel the same way about small bits of London which, for all its lovable characters, remains faceless - bigger than the people who populate it. But cities grow, and maybe one day Leeds and Bradford will overlap and merge and we'll have a big faceless northern city. Right now they have distinct characters. If you read DC comics then Bradford is to Leeds what Gotham is to Metropolis. More industrial than commercial. Buildings closer together, almost leaning inwards, clutters of statuesque masonry casting dark shadows upon the streets below. At dusk the starlings swarm around the town hall clock-tower like iron filings around a magnet, before settling on ledges of stone and strips of lead, blackened by years of soot from the surrounding mills and turned green by the elements. It makes me think of bats and belfries. As do the students. Many a Nick Cave fan amongst them.

Anyway, apart from the obvious curry houses and delicatessens, it means you can get Polish beer. Try it. I was getting stuck into a Zywiec when Tim showed up at ten to three. Zeds had been open since Monday - during the day that is, when it functions as a cafe bar. It wasn't as busy as usual so Tim and I took a regular table rather than go through to the office.

"You sleep any?" I enquired.

"Some."

I gave Tim the typed report. He began overplaying the importance of my leads. I think he just wanted to feel we were achieving something. I managed to persuade him that shooting up some Manchester drug dealers and carpet-bombing Dorset might be an over reaction.

He sighed and shrugged his shoulders. You could hear his muscles creaking.

"We're opening tonight. You gonna be here?" he asked.

"Too right."

I didn't think for one minute that they had finished with Zeds. *Something* was going to happen and I wanted to be close by when it did.

So come the evening there I was. As I've said, Thursdays are relatively quiet and this was no exception but things were ticking over nicely. I had worried earlier in the day that our reputation had been damaged to the extent that business was affected. Naa, things were okay.

At one point I spent a couple of hours in the office. I was looking through phone bills and receipts and staff records. I knew that there was some way in which inside information was being used against us. I looked for anything that stood out - phone calls clustering around recent events, any to Dorset? Any employees with suspicious backgrounds? That was a laugh - try and find a bouncer without one.

I was floundering.

Something from the deepest recess of my mind was telling me that I was missing something but it wouldn't tell me what. Hate that.

When I got back on the floor. Danny said to me, "Seen your little mate in tonight."

He meant Kelp. With Danny you could tell he wanted to say something racist but he wouldn't have dared. These ex-army guys are nothing without an SA80. Even if he did have one I'd take it off him. I'd been practising.

Which part of 'steer clear' hadn't he understood? I looked around but I couldn't see the Boy Wonder. Saved himself a bollocking. Maybe Dan had imagined it.

The rest of the night passed without incident. Or so I thought.

Chapter 12

I awoke to rain drumming the window. The heavy curtains did nothing to muffle the sound. December had arrived and the monsoon season was still upon us. Flood waters had been plaguing Britain and reminding us of how vulnerable we all are.

From my bed I could see part of the window through the side of the curtains and watched the water rolling down the glass. I watched for too long. When I do that it reminds me of one time as a child when someone I didn't know was baby-sitting me in a house I didn't know either. It was odd because my brother and sister weren't there. I didn't understand. I was staring out of a window on the strange scene of a long street I didn't recognise and wondering if my mother was ever coming back. I wasn't crying because the rain was doing it for me. I felt entitled to be upset but I didn't feel safe to show it to a stranger. I fostered the acceptance that comes with powerlessness. It was perhaps the most adult moment I've ever experienced - and I don't think I could have been more than four years old.

How vulnerable we all are.

I wondered if Dorset was underwater?

The cat was creating by the kitchen door. "Me out!" I don't have a cat flap. Waste of time because it won't use them. I sighed and opened the door slightly ajar. The cat nosed out then pulled it's head tortoise-like into it's shoulders and just sat there staring at the rain like it was my fault. That cat does nothing for my self-esteem. Perhaps I should get a dog and bask in its idiotic worship.

I was still thinking about Kelp but had mellowed a little since last night. He'd probably been in under sufferance with a bunch of mates, stopping off before heading up to the Palm Cove or some other dive. On a Thursday night though?

His mobile was switched off so I went over to see him.

He'd want to hear about recent developments even though he wasn't involved in the club investigation any longer.

I gave the door a firm knock and braced myself against the rain - it might be a long wait for him to drag himself out of his pit.

I wasn't prepared for the speed at which the door was opened, nor for who answered.

A girl. Stunning she was. Absolutely.

This must be Kelp's sister, I thought to myself. I stood there. The rain rained some more and not a word would come out of my mouth.

She looked me up and down. A brief assessment.

"You must be Chris O'Brien. Would you like to come in?"

Luckily my feet worked. With supreme effort I managed to speak.

"Yes. Thank you."

King of the snappy comeback.

She told me she was Debra, Kel's sister, up from London. I noticed she said Kel. I'm probably the only one who calls him Kelp. I said that he had mentioned her and it was nice to meet her. Snap out of it O'Brien. Chat required

"So, how did you know who I was?"

"Well, you're a bit old to be one of his other mates..."

Cheers, I thought. Good start. I guessed I was maybe five or six years older than her.

I sat in the first chair that presented itself in my path. It was adjacent to the telly. Couldn't see what was on but I could hear *Trisha's* strident tones issuing forth.

"And you don't look like a policeman either." Kelp used to be in with the proverbial 'bad crowd' and had done his fair share of twocking and credit card fraud. Before my time, but that didn't stop him getting the odd visit on the strength of his former behaviours.

"Oh aye, what do I look like then?" I ventured hopefully.

She looked me up and down again, this time playful, still assessing but now for fun.

79

"Hmm, a social worker, or a nurse maybe?"

Charming. No matter what I wear, or how many hours I spend in the gym, I never manage to look like a tough guy. I'm told there's a softness about my face. I console myself that it encourages people to open up to me. Also, in a fight I tend to be under-estimated - which is always a bonus. Little old non-threatening me. Doesn't make me a babe magnet.

"Actually, I'm a private investigator." Maybe that would work. Intrepid. Windswept and interesting.

"Oh I know. I've had a lot of catching up to do, been out of touch with the family, but you've been just about all I've heard from Kel."

I managed to suppress the urge to say 'all good I hope'. Chat graveyard.

"He not in then?" I said.

"No. Went out last night. Probably at some mate's house."

"Oh." I was really struggling here.

"So, does that mean you're done here? Or would you like a coffee?" She sounded amused. I like it when I amuse people but generally I like it to be intentional.

"Cheers, yeah."

"How do you take it?"

"Black as the night and sweet as a stolen kiss."

"That would be - no milk, two sugars, right?"

"Yeah, Thanks. That how I take it."

Was it fuck how I took it. It's called flirting and I'm normally better at it than this.

I got up and followed her to the small oblong kitchen which attached to the living room. Habit. Best conversations happen when you're not sat facing each other. Hard to be defensive when you're brewing up. More polite too, I thought. Less like being waited on.

The kettle commenced gurgling as soon as she plugged it in. She must have just had one. I glanced back through to the living room and, for sure, there was a half-drunk cup resting on the caramel colour ceramic fire surround. If in doubt, observe. Do what you're used to. Regain a sense of control. The coffee and tea were beside the kettle. The coffee was Douwe Egberts, which is one of my favourite instants. I noticed she put a really big heaped teaspoon into her cup. For the sugar she had to reach up into the kitchen unit. She obviously didn't take sugar either. Maybe only when flirting. As she reached up she exposed a little midriff flesh between the top of her combats and the bottom of her T-shirt. Goddamn.

"Nice view," I ventured.

Making a point of looking out into the small garden that the kitchen backed onto. Yeah, like I meant the garden. Flirting again.

She was smiling and tidying away imaginary strands of hair from her face. She didn't seem shy. She just seemed to be playing the same game as me but with a greater degree of subtlety.

We repaired to the living room and Debra knelt down by the fire, where her coffee was. I was daring and, rather than return to the chair, knelt too.

"Private detective, eh? Have you got a licence?" she said. It had to come.

"Don't need one in this country. Just got to stay the right side of the law."

"I don't suppose you've got a gun then?" She was being playful again.

"No, I'm just pleased to see you." I almost winced as I said it. Too playful.

She laughed like she was genuinely amused but also like she'd heard it a thousand times before. Skilful. I made a mental note to take lessons from her on how to do that.

"Are you any good, Mr Detective? Kel really sings your praises."

"Naa. Generally, it takes me both hands to find me arse." Self-deprecation, humour, and a reference to my arse. All in one sentence. Flirt-miester.

"Maybe I could lend you a hand?" She giggled. I was instantly grateful to her for lowering the tone too. I sensed that was exactly why she'd said it. Make me feel more comfortable.

But I wasn't feeling too comfortable. There was nothing that I wanted more at that moment than to remain in this lovely girl's company but I had to reel it back in somehow. I felt slightly intimidated and that made me feel ridiculous. Also, the back of my mind was ticking over on where the hell Kelp was.

In an effort to raise the tone I asked her about the degree she was doing and about life down in London. We name-checked a few places we both knew down there and I told her about when I'd used to live in Kilburn. We made polite conversation.

As we knelt there our knees were almost touching.

I shifted position and went cross-legged. Quite a flirty way to sit, demonstrating both one's physical flexibility and sensitive spiritual side. It also bought our faces slightly closer together.

Then she went and mirrored me, but pulled off a full lotus position. Skill. We were really face to face now.

I carried on talking, about what I do not know. If I left any gaps in what I was saying then Trisha would intrude from the background. The topic was, incidentally, something to do with people who'd had sex on the first occasion they'd met and were now 'red hot lovers'. Lord. My voice was starting to get hoarse.

Debra had pretty much stopped talking herself and was just nodding at me, smiling the most beautiful smile this side of anywhere, making me do all the talking now and watching me get all hot and bothered. Enjoying herself. Then she said it, "Kiss me." Halfway between a request and an order.

Heavens to Murgatroyd.

I leaned forward and kissed her. It was the right thing to

do. Either that or get up and leave. Can't see you blushing when you kiss them.

It was a good kiss.

She leaned slowly backwards. Not pulling away but forcing me to push forward if I wanted to maintain the contact. I did. Coming out of my semi-lotus and basically climbing on top of her as she gently lay down on the floor. Blood was now rushing to my head, and other places. We kept kissing. Longer, wetter, more passionate.

The rest of our bodies start to follow the movement of the kissing. Soon we were pushing against each other with such pressure that it would have been unpleasantly painful in any other context.

She gripped the back of my hair in her fist and pulled me even closer into her. She spoke into my ear. Softly but without a hint of shyness.

"I'm on the pill, and I know I'm clean. You?"

I gulped.

"I'm clean...but I'm not on - " She bit my bottom lip to shssh me. Ouch.

I decided I wasn't prepared to be at it on the living room floor if there was a chance that Kelp would walk in - no matter how keen he'd been for me to meet her. I hefted Debra into my arms and began carrying her upstairs, managing not to bump her head on the ceiling or her feet on the bannister. Hours spent in the gym paying off after all.

At the top of the stairs I footed open the door I knew to be to the spare room. She might have been stopping in her mum's room for all I knew but I didn't want to be disrespectful. Didn't want to lose my hard-on either, so stop thinking about her mum. Stop it now.

We rolled onto the bed and we did it.

It was wild. It was like an explosion that just kept on exploding. It was also tender. It was everything between wild and tender. It was obvious that Debra had inherited all the genes for physical co-ordination in that family and there had been something so predatorial in her behaviour that made the surrendering all the more sweet when it finally came. God, was it good.

Afterwards we lay close together and entwined. Washed up by waves and stranded on some strange shore. I felt distinctly high. Everything was vivid, colourful, fresh. The paint on the walls, the texture of the bed's fabric. The world had been removed, cleansed in spring water and white musk, then replaced carefully around us.

My eyes were wide and a knot in my stomach, which I hadn't even been aware of before, was gone. Every time I tried to speak, even just a little word like 'phew' or 'wow', Debra would kiss me brutally on the mouth to stop me. It became a game, we were soon both giggling and the pressing of bodies together commenced once more.

Then came the knock at the door.

Debra pushed herself up like an arching cat for a quick view through the window then, in one smooth motion, rolled me away from her and was at the side of the bed, almost already dressed and off down the stairs.

Alone in the room now it was my turn to look out of the window. In the street a police car. Kelp. Something terrible had happened.

The world around me darkened, the knot in my stomach was back.

The rain just rained.

Chapter 13

I could barely draw breath until I heard that Kelp was still alive. The news was not good by any standards, he was in hospital and 'unconscious' - I noticed the policeman didn't say 'coma'. I felt a confused mixture of horror, guilt and relief. Debra looked as calm as you could expect but she seemed a million miles away from me. The officer asked me politely if I could contact the local CID as soon as I was able to. I made some sort of noise and nodded.

I drove to the hospital as fast as I could without causing any accidents. Debra sat in the passenger seat in silence that was difficult to read. My mouth kept pushing out odd single words of shock, anger and fear. I noticed that she wasn't kissing me to shut me up.

We parked as near to the 'All Wards' entrance as I could and just ran straight in. You don't think about obtaining a valid ticket in those circumstances and hospitals would do well to think about that.

We arrived at the reception of ICU and Debra explained to the staff that she was next of kin in her mother's absence. I could see Kelp from where I was. He was not sitting up. A girl in a light blue tunic and trousers seemed to be finishing up around his bedside, then she started wheeling away an ECG machine. I caught her eye and she gave me a smile. I think it was an 'everything's going to be okay' smile. I guess it was something that he wasn't on a permanent monitor.

We both went over to the bed. Debra sat and slid her hand gently under his. There was a canula on the back of his hand that led to a saline drip, no plasma or haemoglobin - which again was encouraging. His face was swollen from some contusions but there didn't appear to be anything that wouldn't heal up nicely - I couldn't see any of the nasty lacerations that would leave scars. Except for his right eye. It was patched and bandaged and he could have lost it entirely for all I knew. I took the chart from the end of his bed that held a record of his physical observations. It was very neat and easy to read but then this was intensive care. Everything seemed fairly normal - for a traumatised body, that is - he did not seem to be at death's door. They didn't keep ECG or EEG readings on this chart, not that I'd have been able to interpret them if they did. But I wanted to know if his brain activity was 'normal'. I looked over at Debra but she was just looking at her little brother. I went off to collar a medic.

There was one at the nurse's station. She was leaning heavily on the counter and reading some charts. I introduced myself and enquired after Kelp.

"He's doing well, all his signs are good. Opiate levels are way down now. We just waiting for him to wake up."

"Opiate levels?"

"Heroin overdose. Maybe he took it to numb the pain of that beating he received."

"Pure?"

"Good God, no. Just the regular crappy stuff. Pure would have killed him. It looks like it was his first time, though?" She frowned, asking me the question.

"To my knowledge, yes."

Those bastards. The thought of them forcing the drugs into him and then working him over with minimal resistance made me want to kill. I did hope for Kelp's and Mark's sake that it had happened that way round though. Less painful. I took a deep breath.

"His eye?"

"It's intact. Don't know what else yet until he regains consciousness. We don't think the retina's detached but there's some scratching on the cornea and he doesn't want it infected."

She glanced past me and smiled.

"Looks like he's with us. Thought it wouldn't be too long."

I looked over and he was indeed beginning to stir. Debra was stroking his arm. I thanked the doctor for her time.

"I'll be with him in a minute. You go tell him we need the bed." She winked and then ran off after a nurse who'd just passed us.

You had to admire them.

He was pretty groggy but he recognised us and said, "So you've met, then?"

We both thought that was a riot but suppressed the laughter because you could see from his painful wincing that he wanted to laugh too. I told him to rest and said that we could talk about what happened later. Obviously I wanted to know it all there and then in every detail but it wouldn't have been right. A different doctor and a nurse came round, tested various responses which seemed to be tiring enough for poor Kelp.

Then the CID guy with the thick glasses turned up. Kelp whispered to me, "Do you want me to tell him anything?" I don't think he was bothered what he was saying but a whisper was all he could manage.

"Tell him everything you can, but don't tire yourself out. Send him away if you've had enough. See you later, Bro."

Kelp made a movement that would have been a nod under healthier conditions. Debra kissed him on the forehead.

"Don't hassle him," I said to Glasses.

He gave me a look that told me not to tell him his job. Then he said, "Phone Hadley."

We left.

When we came out of reception there were two security guards just starting to fix a clamp to the offside front wheel of my car.

"Okay lads," I said "Save you a job. We're just on our way."

One of them shook his head and sucked air through his

teeth the way people do when they really want to piss you off. The other one said,

"You have failed to obtain a valid ticket. If you would like the clamp to be removed you will need to pay a fine of £40."

He had one of those high pitched voices that some Yorkshire men do. He had the mullet and moustache look that went with the voice. The other one had thinning grey hair and a lot of scar tissue around the eyes like an ex-boxer. Middle-aged thugs. Security is not a high paying job. You pay peanuts you get monkeys. Or in their case, gorillas.

"Come on, you haven't even put it on yet! I'll pay for the ticket if you like. We were in a hurry…"

The silent partner grinned. The teeth he had previously sucked air through were put on display. Not pretty. An ugly gorilla.

The other one turned his head away from me and back to his clamp. He started to repeat his rehearsed sentence whilst his back was turned to me. An ill-mannered gorilla.

"You have failed to obtain a valid ticket. If you would like the clamp…"

"Clamp… my… arse!" I explained to him.

I had knelt down next to him, placed my hand between the tyre and the clamp and put my face right into his.

He shot up abruptly, almost falling over as he did so. His mate closed in, which helped him regain his composure. I noticed, with a sinking feeling, that the clamp was now partly attached and it would now not simply be a matter of driving away.

"Don't you dare threaten me! We are empowered to remove you from the premises if you obstruct us in the course of our duties."

He was hissing at me now. The silent one was almost leering at me. You could tell that removing people was the favourite part of his duties.

"It will take more than Cannon and fucking Ball to remove me. The only thing you'll be removing, mate, is that clamp."

I rarely get into these sort of confrontations, even as a part-time bouncer. Normally I just blarney my way out but my body was still on an adrenaline rollercoaster that had started with the knock on the door. Part of my mind was ashamed of myself for displacing my anger onto these people I had never met - jobsworths though they were. The other part of my mind was busy justifying my righteous indignation and, since it had my adrenalized body as an ally, was winning.

O'Brien Vs. Bradford Health Authority. Again. I'll tell you about it sometime.

Ugly shifted slightly closer. I saw his shoulders bunch and knew he was seconds away from making a move on me. Bring it on, King Kong.

At that point Debra stepped up. I'd almost forgotten she was there and the shame part of me grew instantly larger. My behaviour was far from impressive.

"What did you call me?"

She directed this at the one who'd been doing the talking. There was a hardness in her voice that made my threats sound hollow.

"I beg your pardon, Miss?"

You could see his cogs turning, trying to work out which part of the security handbook he should be quoting at this stage of the proceedings. Coming up blank. Does not compute.

"You just called me a black bitch. Your language and manner is totally unacceptable and I want to speak to your manager immediately."

Her voice was raised but without sounding at all out of control. Passers-by were beginning to pay attention, a large group of them Asian, and I wondered if she had timed her attack with their arrival.

"I n…n... never," he stammered.

"I'm not surprised that you attempt to deny it. I do have witnesses."

I nodded. She was so totally believable in her manner that I'm sure she could have hauled any one of the growing audience over and they would have sworn blind they had heard the racial slur.

For a moment, Ugly looked like he wanted to hit her to shut her up. I think that was the extent of his repertoire.

"But I - " seethed Mullet, who had now turned into Blakey off *On the Buses*.

"Your manager. Now."

A murmur of appreciation from the crowd behind us. The British Public vs. Officialdom. Who loves a clamper?

I was absolutely grinning my ass off.

"Well, if you *are* just on your way..."

Debs continued to act like she wouldn't be happy with anything less than their instant dismissal. Blakey knelt down and removed the clamp purely for something to occupy his trembling hands and Ugly just walked away. He was off to hit something. Anything.

The audience dispersed as we got in the car and drove off. We were giggling like school kids again.

"Well, China, the art of fighting without fighting. What did you think of that?"

"I think you're a black bitch."

She smiled wide.

"I hate to play the race card, it erodes the fabric of society, but sometimes it be all we gots, you know what I'm say'n?" For the last part of the sentence she lapsed into a hilarious ghetto drawl.

"I wouldn't sweat it, those two looked pretty eroded anyway."

I was so grateful to her for relieving the tension. I felt like she had every right to hate me for putting her little brother in danger. I also felt like her hating me would be unbearable, the worst thing that could happen in the world. Yet here she was saving me from making a tosser of myself in a public car park. That is some kind of woman.

She rifled my glove box for a cassette. It's all Rap and TV themes in there. She pulled out Public Enemy's 'Fear of a Black Planet', made a little whooping noise, and stuck it on. We sang along to the chorus of '911 is a Joke' at the top of our voices as I drove. It was like we'd known each other ten years.

There was one long stretch of road on the way home where I shifted up into fifth gear and didn't have to change down for a couple of minutes. During that time our fingers managed to find each other, and we held hands.

Chapter 14

We got back to the house and she phoned her mum. Christ knows what time it was over there. Debra outlined the whole situation in a soft calming tone whilst I stood there like a spare part. The last thing she said was "Yeah, he's here" and held the handset out towards me as my heart skipped a beat.

There was a tremulous quality in Mrs. Prentice's voice that made it sound like she had been crying but was beginning to pull it back. I was all apologies but she wasn't having any of it. She sees me as some sort of stabilizing influence in her son's life. I'd have preferred her to be mad at me. When I told her I'd catch whoever did this I'd have preferred her to say "don't talk shit" rather than "I know you will."

When I'd finished up, Debra had made me another coffee. I didn't dare ask for milk. What a way to start a relationship. She fixed me with a look that was direct and challenging but there was compassion in there too. A bit like a schoolteacher attending to a struggling pupil.

"You blame yourself. There's no need."

"I feel responsible for this."

She shook her head.

"You feel responsible for *him*. You're not. You'd have protected him if you could. You'll avenge him if you can. You had no control over what happened - that must make it scary, but it's also what makes it okay. How you act from now on is what matters."

It was exactly what I would have said to anyone else if the tables were turned. Except I'd maybe have beaten around the bush a little more.

"But you know all that anyway," she said. Like she'd read my mind.

"You seem to know a lot about me…" Apart from how I really take my coffee.

"We're alike." She shrugged.

"You could be right. I feel like I know you, but I don't know anything about you."

"Well, you won't have heard much from Kel, he knows very little about me. But from what he's told me about you there's a lot I can identify with."

"How so?" I was interested.

"You're into Chinese culture. Philosophy, medicine, martial arts?"

I nodded.

"Do you have a *Shaolin* prayer?"

I did. I recited it for her and swelled with pride as I did so.

"Be master of the hard ways and the soft ways. Be powerful from within and without. Be of wisdom and also of deeds. Know how to hurt and also how to heal."

She smiled but it was a serious smile.

"Then you have a code. So do I. That makes us alike. Not many of us around."

She was right. For all the opinionated people I've met, there were very few who would stand up for what they believed in. For all the 'protesters' I knew, there were very few who actually *believed* in anything, save for whatever ready made 'cause' they happened to be following that week.

"What code do you have then?"

"*Bushido*. The Japanese arts." There was pride in her voice too.

Culture's a funny thing. Here we were, English-born Irish, English-born West Indian, both looking to the East for lifestyle advice.

"Kelp said something about you kicking my ass."

"He doesn't really know what I can do. I did Ju-jitsu at school but it's only since I've been away that I've really studied."

I was starting to get a sense of how much she was revealing. This seemed to be stuff she wouldn't normally talk about. I've got stuff like that too; stuff where you think 'who'd listen?'. I realized that Debra was probably a very guarded person most of the time. She probably didn't appear to be much of a fun person to those around her. With me she was being less guarded. That made me feel special. Perhaps I could return the favour and bring out her fun side. No chance of doing that under the present circumstances though.

"I suppose your code means that you want to avenge your brother too?"

"The human part of me wants to. The code means that I'll follow through and do what I can."

Wasn't sure what I thought about that.

At any other time we'd have carried on talking into the small hours, and God knows I needed it, but there was so much to do and it was making me jittery. She could tell.

We kissed as I left and it was awkward. Well, I was. She wasn't.

I went to my office because it was nearer than home. The first call I made was to DS Hadley. He wasted no time with pleasantries.

"My guvnor has told me to make it clear to you, once more, not to intefere with our investigation."

"Right."

"And I want you to tell me anything you know."

"Bit of a mixed message there, Phil," I pointed out.

"Have you had any calls to that reward hotline of yours?"

"Only piss-takes."

"Any leads at all?"

"Have you?"

"Not your business, O'Brien, as I've said."

"I'm going to spend the rest of the day talking to Zed staff to find out who they saw Kelp leaving with. I'm going to talk to Kelp this evening if he's well enough. I bet you've already done the same. I'm not obstructing you in any way."

"Your Kelp didn't tell DC Green much at all. Did you tell him to keep quiet?"

"No. I told him to be honest. Blows to the head tend to shag your short term memory. Or weren't you aware of that? Your man better not have given him a hard time…"

"Calm down will you. We both want the same thing."

"Well, fine. Just don't expect me to sit on my hands. I'll tell you anything I think is relevant. It would be good if you could do the same."

"You know I can't, so don't ask."

"Well, grand." I was gritting my teeth.

"O'Brien, if you want to be useful then I think Marconi might appreciate your psychiatric skills. He's going to pieces."

Yeah. Tim had been doing his best to be Trevini's buffer zone on this one. He was generally a cool customer but his skill was in facing situations of immediate threat and resolving them on the spot. He was obviously not built for the grinding slog of investigating an unknown cause. Maybe I wasn't either.

"Thanks for your concern, Phil. Any of your officers need their arses wiping while I'm at it?"

He chuckled, which actually helped to break my foul mood a little.

"You do what you need to do, O'Brien. Just don't break the law and don't hold out on us." And he was gone.

I phoned Tim. He's not the easiest guy in the world to be supportive towards. So I just kept agreeing with him that we'd "get these bastards." He told me that Darren had been the only one on the door to see Kelp leave. That cut my afternoon's workload down a bit but I'd have preferred more to go on.

I phoned Darren. He was more helpful than I thought he'd be. Mostly he only pays attention to the ladies. Kelp had left on his own but Daz had seen him talking to two lads at the top of the stairs and, because of being questioned about it, he'd managed to remember that these lads had left only a little while before Kelp. His description was both early twenties, dressed smart casual. One had 'big hair'. I got him to compare them to people off the telly. One looked like Jonathan Creek - but hard. The other had 'gladiator' hair, very dark black, and sharp, weasely features. He told me if he saw them again he'd have 'em. I said thanks.

I went back to visit Kelp. He was now in a regular medical ward but he had a side room all to himself. I mainly did the talking, filling him in on everything I'd been up to since I last saw him. He seemed to like the bit about the gun. Obviously hadn't had any sense beaten into him. I asked him if he could tell me anything. He shook his head fractionally but winced painfully as he did so.

"I remember going to the club. I'm sorry…"

I held my hand up in a stop sign.

"The next thing I remember is struggling," he croaked, "in a room that wasn't like a room, small, dark, loud…the last thing I remember was being on the floor."

The room I was picturing was either a shed or the back of a van. I asked him if he knew where he'd been found, he said no. I told him not to worry.

"I know I was drugged, and also I dreamt about being a tiger. I think it was something you taught me."

I had taught him a *Qi Gong* exercise once. You emulate the posture of a tiger and it's supposed to tonify your liver energies. I probably jokingly told him it was a hangover cure.

"So you saved me, man…"

I wanted to scream and shout at him. Tell him it was due to blind luck and medical expertise that he was still alive. Not some poxy exercise. I didn't have the heart so I just shrugged.

"Debs is coming over later. I think she wants to know what's going on."

I knew what was coming next and I wanted him to save his voice. I sighed and told him to tell her whatever she wanted to know.

It was looking like there would be three separate investigations going on.

I left the portable stereo and CDs I'd bought for him and walked off down the long bland hospital corridor. There was a pub just down the way that had always been a good stop-off after hospital visits. They'd have an open fire going this time of year.

I walked in and saw the two security guards from that morning stood at the bar. I kept on walking and straight out the back. They didn't deserve my anger.

I had beer in the fridge.

And I sat and drank that beer. And I tried to think of the morning with Debra. So far away. It was nearly time to get to Zeds, if that was where I was going to go. I still wasn't actually on duty, but I felt like I should be doing something. Maybe I could invite Debra over to see the club?

Then the phone shocked me from my musings. The call was from Trevini's residence. It was the man himself.

"Chris, can you come here please." His voice was hollow and full of fear. "Francesca is missing."

His 15-year-old daughter. I felt like I'd been kicked in the guts and I realised that would only be a fraction of how he was feeling. A coldness spread over me.

"What happened?"

"The school rang just right now. She was last seen early this afternoon."

That would make it maybe six hours now she had been missing. Francesca was away at boarding school. It was a link none of us had made, none of us would think to or want to. She was an untouchable princess far removed from the sordid goings-on up North. Before, it was a coincidence that didn't warrant a mention. With the benefit of hindsight you might call it gross negligence. Where was her boarding school?

Fucking Dorset.

Chapter 15

I drove faster than I should have to Trevini's but, in the dark, it was the kind of country road where you could see most vehicles quite a way off by their lights. I thought about Francesca on the way. She was Mr. Trevini's only child and I knew her fairly well; I'd even been to her school once before early on in the year. She'd dearly wanted to go to a concert - Rage Against the Machine at the Brixton Academy - and I'd been asked if I would chaperone her. Apparently, out of all the people he employed, I had looked the part and was considered trustworthy. I was honoured. Tim would have been trustworthy but wouldn't have looked the part. For a bouncer, he remains ignorant about modern music. The rumour is he thinks Basement Jaxx is a discount clothing store in Leeds.

Since then, I'd chatted to her at Trevini's barbecues and we'd taken her dog, Yoda, for a couple of walks on Ilkley moor. She'd told me once I was 'cool'. I liked her. Whoever was behind all this was going to suffer when I got hold of them.

I ground to a halt in the gravel driveway, scattering the edge of the dark lawn with tiny pebbles, and went straight in. It was unlocked like before. Trevini, Tim and a guy straight out of the Grecian 2000 advert were there. He introduced himself as Geoff Robertshaw, Solicitor. He had been there earlier regarding other matters when Trevini had received the phone call and had hung around to lend moral support. He seemed effusively glad at my arrival and appeared to be very apprehensive in the presence of Tim who sat in a leather armchair with his head in his hands.

There is no Mrs. Trevini, in case you're wondering. She died of cancer before I'd ever met Trevini. I've seen pictures of her and she looked like she was a lovely person.

There was more to the atmosphere than just the tension I

would have expected. There was a different kind of uneasiness too. It centered around Tim. A glance at the normally tidy desk showed that its contents were stacked in one pile, as if they'd all just been picked up off the floor. I guessed that Tim had swept them off in a fit of rage. Feelings of anger and impotence hung heavy in the air of the room. Now there was quiet embarrassment too. It didn't help.

I became the focus of attention and that felt okay. I touched Trevini on the upper arm, there was a pause, and then the usual hug. No back-slapping this time though.

I phoned the school and spoke to one of the security personnel, asked her to check some things for me and phone back. Then I sat down and tried to get as much info as I could out of those present. I had my cool, calm and collected head on and everyone seemed glad of it.

The school phoned back. Efficient. I said a lot of uh huhs and thank yous and did quite a bit of nodding for the benefit of my immediate audience. When I'd finished and hung up they all looked at me expectantly and I held forth.

"From what I can gather, Fran left the school of her own free will at around 3.00pm. The receptionist got the impression that she was just popping out. She had a small rucksack with her and it also appears that some personal items - toothbrush, make up and so forth are missing."

I paused for breath whilst everyone continued staring at me.

"It doesn't look like kidnapping," I pronounced. There seemed to be the tiniest release of tension in the room as I said that. "Plus the fact that we haven't heard from anyone to that effect. It's not odd for Fran to stay at a friend's house over the weekend, is it?"

I looked at Trevini and he nodded.

"But what is odd is not to let anyone know where she was going. The school's pretty strict about things like that?"

Trevini nodded again. A little tension crept back into the air.

"Even odder that she made it sound like she was going to be back soon but seems to have intended to be out at least overnight. Unless she's just not thinking at all, it makes it look like she wants us to worry. Why would she do that?"

"I feel like I don't know her mind so well," said Trevini "She does not phone so much these days. She is distant. Perhaps she is just growing up."

"So she may be unhappy?" She had seemed happy the last time I saw her, during the summer.

Still silence, awkwardness and attention from everyone. Waiting for a conclusion. Waiting for me to say - "This is what we do". How did I land this role? Being the focus of attention had become a little less comfortable.

"The school will contact the local police in the morning if she hasn't returned. Do you want me to go down and investigate too?"

"Yes please, Chris, would you?"

"Of course. I'll leave tonight." I wanted to be as reassuring to Trevini as I possibly could. Also, if I wanted to make any difference I should conduct my interviews before the police did theirs. And if Francesca turned up bleary eyed the next morning, I'd be there to give her a roasting.

But I did feel uncomfortable that this was leading me away from the local goings on, important as this was to sort out, even if it was just a coincidence. I didn't know if I wanted it to be a coincidence or not. All I knew was that I wanted to protect those I loved and I wanted to find and destroy anyone who was a threat to them. I just didn't know which part of the country I needed to be in to do all that most effectively.

Mr. Robertshaw made his apologies and sympathetic noises and left. I got on the phone to a hotel in Blandford Forum, near the school, and asked if it would pose any problems for me to turn up in the early hours of the morning. Trevini said from behind me: "Tell them, money no object." I've always wanted to say that but chose not to at this particular time.

Then I phoned Mrs. Danvers who lives across the road from me and keeps a key, apologised for the lateness of the hour, and asked if she'd feed the cat whilst I was away.

Never a problem.

Tim, a little brighter now, asked if he should come too. I wanted to tell him to go on holiday but it wouldn't have been well received.

"No, mate. You're needed up here aren't you?"

He looked pleased at the vote of confidence. I suggested to Tim that he contact the local nick and appraise them. They may consider it significant, they may not. I told them both I'd keep in touch every step of the way, and then off I went, calling back to the house for clothes. Something smart for the school, everything else just warm, comfortable and nondescript. Surveillance gear. If in doubt, which, as a PI, you so often are, it's what you wear. I phoned the hospital ward and asked if Kelp could receive text messages on the ward. The nurse laughed and said that, although mobiles weren't allowed on the ward, he already had one member of staff going out to the car park to send and receive for him. I said to tell him I'd keep in touch.

The cat looked at me like it knew I might be gone for a while. It came over and head-bumped my leg. Then it went and sat behind the curtain and stared out the front window. That's what it does always before I go away for a while and I never know whether it's acceptance or petulance.

I drove off down dark and empty streets.

Chapter 16

I hit the M1 before midnight. I'd picked up some tapes to keep me company on the drive down. Everything Tom Waits had done over the last decade. Dark, brutal, disjointed, almost psychotic. It suited my mood. I've driven down to that part of the country a couple of times before and, on the single lane A350, it's possible to get stuck behind an artic at any time of the day or night. I don't think I could have coped with that. Luckily, for the last leg, I remembered the top road that takes you past Compton Abbas airfield and clocked up what was certainly a personal best. I very rarely speed because I don't actually enjoy it but I managed to hit 90 a few times for my sins. I arrived at the hotel at around 3.45 a.m.

A couple of members of staff were waiting up for me and gave a good reception, whilst respectfully requesting that I keep the noise to a minimum when retiring to bed. Not that I was in the mood for a party anyway. I set the alarm on my mobile for 8.00 a.m. and went out like a light, which was pretty good under the circumstances. The luxury of clean sheets is a powerful hypnotic.

Good hotels are busy all the year round and this place was fairly bustling by the time I got down to breakfast. It was self-service but excellent nonetheless. The scrambled egg was neither watery nor tinged with grey and the bacon came in a choice of either crispy or floppy. Choice of all the newspapers too. The proper ones. That would have been me sorted all morning if I didn't have work to do.

After eating I headed back upstairs and re-dressed into the gear that I hadn't wanted to drop any food on. Base loafers, fawn Chinos, pale blue polo shirt and, the star of the show: a navy blue cashmere blazer by Aquascutum that I'd taken in part payment for a job at a mill shop where some labels had been going amiss. I checked myself in the mirror.

Chris O'Brien – detective to the aristocracy. Either that or a right merchant banker.

The school was an imposing building but with an elegance that said 'Girls Boarding School' in a plummy voice. There was none of the austerity that I remembered about any of the public schools in the North that our comprehensive used to lose rugby matches to. But I guess that if the only bit you get to see is the changing rooms then maybe the impression is skewed. I'd been here before but only to pick Fran up. I had never got any further than the lobby that time.

I had requested to speak to some of Francesca's room-mates and the school was ready for me; I was ushered briskly into a large office room by the receptionist. Left to my own devices for a few moments in a comfortable leather chair, studded with brass rivets. Floor to ceiling bookshelves, and none of your paperbacks. Bought by the yard? I took a deep breath and tried to soak in the atmosphere. It was a clear day and the winter sun was pushing its way through the mist of the morning sky, piercing the tall latticed window and dappling the fine burgundy carpet with a patch of tentative light. Momentarily, I was joined by three young girls and a chaperone, around my age and just as smartly dressed, who introduced herself as Miss Culliver. The three girls with her were introduced as Daphne, Penelope and Cordelia. No word of a lie.

I thanked them for their help in advance, trying to ooze as much charm as I could muster, then kicked in with the questions. What were Fran's normal patterns of movement for a weekend? Had she been acting differently lately? When I asked if she had a boyfriend there was a slight uneasiness and shared glances before they all responded in the negative. I'd come back to that.

At my request we all went up to see her bedroom. I had expected a classic dormitory but was mistaken. Theirs was a short, oak-panelled corridor housing four separate bedrooms, one really large bathroom, and also a communal study area that was equipped with both a large screen telly, a microwave and a kettle. The bedrooms themselves were really quite small by comparison to the opulent corridor and it felt a bit of a squash getting us all in. The girls were loosening up a bit now and starting to suppress giggles. Still, I wasn't getting the impression they were hiding anything as such. It seemed like they were disappointed. At a loss as to why she had run out on them like this without confiding anything. She was off having fun somewhere and they weren't. At least they were able to confirm that some clothes, including her favourite dress, were missing. *Cherche le boyfriend*, methinks.

Her diary was also missing. No surprise there. From one of her draws I took some receipts that I would examine in more detail later. We repaired to the plush office room and I broached the subject of boyfriends in general in what I hoped was a disarming manner. The chaperone frowned. It was probably school policy for her to do so at the mention of the word.

"Ladies...if Fran had a boyfriend, is that something you'd expect to know about?"

They exchanged glances again. The coyness that had been cute to start with was beginning to piss me off.

"I'm not interested in getting anyone into trouble and I'm sure Miss Culliver isn't either." I paused and she made a weak nodding movement. "I'm only concerned with Fran's safety. Is there *anything* you can tell me that might help?"

More uneasy looks, like they weren't sure whether to let me into their gang, but thankfully Cordelia piped up and saved me from storming off and taking my bat and ball home.

"Well, we've suspected something." She sounded oh-so-serious. "We haven't seen as much of her on evenings and at the weekends."

I raised my eyebrows towards the heavens. I couldn't help it. I hoped it didn't show. What did they think I'd been asking about earlier? I think I did well not to groan.

"And there was one time in town..." she continued,

warming to her theme, "we saw her getting into a car. I don't think she saw us."

"Did you ask her about it afterwards?"

"We wanted to." The other two nodded. "We kept waiting for her to say something but she didn't. If she was keeping something secret from us we didn't want to get her angry."

Yeah, that'd be right. I already had Fran down as the queen of the corridor. That fiery Italian temperament. The info was a start but I was going to have to do some leg work on this.

"Do you think you could identify the car?" I asked gingerly, not holding out much hope, wishing right now I was in a mixed comprehensive.

The other two looked round at Daphne, who smiled triumphantly.

"Aston Martin DB7 Vantage." She said. I watched her smile broaden.

"Gosh, I bet you can hear him coming." That got a giggle from the others, a frown from the chaperone, but Daphne played it straight down the line.

"Indeed you can. 6.0 litre V12 engine. Delivers 420 bhp and 400lbs of torque."

"Daffers, you really know your automobiles," I said approvingly.

She gave me a mixture of shy and pleased.

"Daddy works for Cosworth."

Yeah, that's right, she said Daddy. Breeding.

"I'm down for a TVR when I'm 17. What do you drive?"

Help.

"An Escort at the moment."

At the moment. That was good, O'Brien. Make it sound like you're on the waiting list for a Ferrari or something. Stop trying to impress the schoolgirls, why don't you?

"Oh, a Cossie?"

Phew. I didn't answer. Let her think what she wants.

"I think you'd call the colour 'racing green'," volunteered Penelope. Daphne was hogging the action.

"Thanks Pen, that's helpful."

Daphne and I shared a brief knowing look. British Racing Green. Actually, it was unlikely to matter if it was Day-Glo pink or monkey-shit brown. There weren't many around. You'd hear it way before you saw it and you'd know it when and if you did see it.

Sex on wheels. In fact, if it *was* pink then Freud would have an absolute field day.

I told them they'd all been most helpful and the girls filed out of the room. Leaving me and Miss Jean Brodie together at last.

"Thanks for your help. This can't be easy for the school. I would suspect you'll be going through the same routine with the local police this afternoon."

"Yes. They've said they'll be over. I'm down for the same duty later. I doubt that the girls will find the police anything like as charming as you though." She smiled and all of a sudden she was a human being. She had been doing a job, playing a role. She wasn't just some monster fashioned out of tweed. Not bad looking either. Eyelashes to die for.

"Perhaps I could check back in with you later. In case the girls do come up with anything that they couldn't manage this morning?"

"Oh, I think I can go one better than that." The smile again. Mischievous this time.

"Do tell." There was something about her manner that made me think she might just be winding me up but I was in 'leave no stone unturned' mode.

"I've seen that car before. And I've seen the driver." She didn't say it in a sing-song voice, but you could almost imagine that she had.

I just carried on looking at her. I didn't fancy saying 'do tell' again. I felt like tapping my foot or whistling but I have highly polished social skills.

She explained that she had seen this person get out of the flash car and speak to a person that she knew. She gave a reasonable description of the guy. Tall, lean, handsome, well groomed, Hugh Grant hair. Makes you sick doesn't it? As if the car wasn't enough. I wanted to know more.

"That's a start. Lets hear more about the person that you do know."

"Listen," she said. Her tone became hushed. "I'm telling you this, but I won't be telling the police."

"Why's that?" I gave her quizzical. She cleared her throat:

"The person he was speaking to is my dealer." She gave a shame-faced look; downcast eyes, shuffling feet. But over-acting, loving it. Proud of her naughtiness, turned on by danger.

I held up my hand in a 'slow down' gesture.

"Okay. First things first. Your secret's safe with me. I'm grateful for the information, but why are you telling me this?"

"I can trust you. You've got that look." She smiled again. Prim and proper had totally vanished. Replaced by pure vamp now. Those lashes.

I sometimes think I've got a sign over my head that says 'I play fast and loose'. I'm as virtuous as the next man, but in a room full of people the bad crowd always manage to find me. My sartorial elegance probably wasn't helping either. Dressing as the Marquis of Blandford must send out the message that one is no stranger to a night out with Charlie. Still, a lead is a lead and, lo and behold, we were back to drugs again.

"Can you set up a meeting with your *friend*?" I asked.

"Yes, I can. I generally see him on a Sunday lunchtime."

That was only tomorrow. I was pleased. Until she spoke again.

"But there's something I want you to do for me."

There's always a catch. She told me what she wanted. I didn't like it but I agreed all the same. I suppose it was the

107

least I could do. We set up the meeting for the next day. I gave her a card. Yeah, a straight one, I wasn't pissing about down here. She told me that her name was Jennifer. As I was leaving she said, "How about tonight. Are you free? You could research the local scene with me."

I made my apologies, saying I had other research to do, which I did as it happens. Back at the hotel I was kindly allowed to use their internet connection and did a search on drugs and the local area. Apparently that particular part of Dorset, according to one of the national broadsheets, was flooded with H. Who'd've thought?

I'd also had some account records faxed down to me from Trevini. Francesca had an American Express card that could draw on her Dad's account. He got sent all the statements.

That afternoon I went and introduced myself to the local plod to let them know about my visit to the school. I was invited in through the custody area and a CID guy came downstairs to speak to me. He smelt strongly of shower gel and his hair was damp. I got the impression he may have arrived straight from the rugby club just moments earlier. Apparently Bradford nick had phoned them that morning and given some background on the Trevini thing, told them I'd be coming down and - wait for it - said it would be nice if we could cooperate. Reading between the lines I think they were happy not to tie in Fran's disappearance if they didn't have to and were probably glad to have me out of their way.

"Do you have any real reason to suspect foul play?" he asked me.

"No. I think it's just an unhappy coincidence. Just added stress for my boss." I was conscious of saying boss rather than client. Just another regular working guy. Not some hotshot who picks and chooses his cases. Minimise any antagonism. I wasn't about to go into the tenuous Dorset connection. Tim might well have told Bradford for all I knew. I didn't care.

I started to tell him about my visit to the school but he

stopped me and told me he wasn't interested. Uniform would be handling it. I was pointed over to a lanky young kid who took out his notebook and nodded with pencil poised whilst I gave him everything. Apart from Jennifer Culliver's extra-curricular activities, that is. Do you know, I didn't see his pencil move once.

After I left the station I texted Kelp but it would be a while before I got any reply. I spent the rest of the afternoon scoping the local area – using Fran's card statements as a rough guide to shops where she made purchases and cash points where she made withdrawals. No, I didn't bump into her.

Also kept a look out for the car. Nothing quite as flash. One Porsche Boxster and no end of BMW Roadsters. Should have brought my I-Spy book.

I thought about phoning Debra but couldn't think for the life of me what I would say. A gulf had opened up between us and, worst of all, I knew it was all of my own making. On the back of little sleep the previous night I retired early. I punched a couple of pillows into the approximate shape of a human being and hugged them tight, thinking of her.

Chapter 17

A few times during the night I'd got some stoned text messages off Jennifer. It was a pain because there was no way I was switching my mobile off under the present circumstances. I didn't respond though and she gave up after a while. I'd got one back from Kelp too. He said, *If there b a clue u know O'Brien gon find it. & if he shootin find cuva & get behind it!*

I wondered what the nursing staff thought of him.

I had a closer look at Fran's statements and receipts, matching them up. Three weekends ago she'd drawn some money out from a cashpoint in Kensington, London. There was a Harrods till receipt from the same date. It was for aftershave. It was the only purchase and only withdrawal she had made that entire weekend. I checked with the school and they confirmed she'd been away for the weekend at a friend's in Chelsea.

How does a fifteen-year-old girl, with her own charge card, go to the city for a weekend and manage not to spend any money? Means someone else is doing the purchasing for her. She'll have insisted on returning the compliment – that's where the gift from Harrods came in.

This 'boyfriend', if he existed, was going to have some explaining to do when I got hold of him. A girlfriend below the age of consent, already a possible drug connection, and a flash motor. I wasn't warming to him. I had the contact number in Chelsea but I'd hang fire on it and see if I could find out anything else first.

I met Jennifer as arranged at 11.30 a.m. The place was a pub called The Talbot on one of the major A roads out of town, heading off towards the downs. I had a Rolling Rock by the neck. Ever deluded yourself that extra pale means lower alcohol? Or that bottles get you less pissed than glasses? She had Vodka Martini, which impressed me slightly as I had her down as the Bacardi Breezer type.

"Good night last night?" I enquired as I set the drinks down.

"Mmmm," she said. "You should have joined us."

Her jaw was working slightly, like she was still chemically enhanced. She had on knee-length black boots, a denim skirt and a pink cardigan that clung in all the right places. Topped off with a felt hat that looked like a puffball mushroom. I was in my Timberlands, cargo pants and a Ben Sherman with button-down collar in light blue check. I think we both felt a little more comfortably attired than yesterday.

I got her to tell me some more about the favour she was asking me. She was going to introduce me to her dealer but she also wanted me to have a word with him about something else.

"He's been putting pressure on me to sleep with him."

She wrinkled her nose in disgust but I again detected some hint of pride, like it was still nice to be wanted.

"He not your type?"

"Ugh! Wait till you see him."

"I presume you've said no? Can't you just move on, get another dealer? Do you owe him money?"

"It's not that. He's threatened to tell the school. I don't want that."

"No shit. So, what you want me to do?"

"Can you...warn him off?" She strung out the last three words of the sentence.

I was silent for a while, took a good pull on the bottle. I'm used to having 'a quiet word' with men on this very subject and it's not as troublesome as you might think. Most men are happy to admit defeat. In fact they normally give up at the point the woman says no.

If the woman hasn't said no then it might be that they've found the man's behaviour intimidating and feared the consequences of rejecting him. Even under these circumstances blokes are often genuinely surprised that they've caused such offence and apologies are the order of the day; that's if you don't go in all guns blazing and get them on the defensive. The other reason some women don't say no is that they actually want the drama of getting a man to do it for them. I'm sorry, but it happens.

Then there'll be the small proportion of men who welcome the aggro. Then you've just got to be better at it than them. Or at least more convincing with the verbals.

With proper stalker headcase types even full on leg-breaking isn't guaranteed to work. It just reinforces their self importance. They need locking up.

I'm sure this bloke was just trying it on as a side-line but, to threaten blackmail, he was definitely power-tripping. If drug dealers ever come up with some sort of Code of Conduct then blackmail has got to be a big no-no. Kind of a pot calling kettle black type scenario. Anyway, there was a big chance that I might have to go heavy on him to learn what I wanted to know, so, in for a penny.

"I'm sure I can reason with him on your behalf."

She grinned, resting her hand on my forearm and letting it linger. I don't know if she was grinning at the irony of my statement or just still buzzing from whatever she'd necked last night. She seemed to be getting excited though.

"But you know it's going to mean finding a new dealer, don't you? I can't see him accepting a slap on the wrist and offering you a discount for his cheek."

"Oh, that's all sorted, darling. As of last night." She gave my arm a squeeze.

We drank up and left. She directed me a little further out of town on the A road, then off on a minor road past a small hamlet of cottages. Back onto another busy A road, then off that through a confusing set of lights and into a seriously large car park, perhaps about an eighth full of articulated lorries, in front of a honest to goodness transport caff. One storey, glass fronted, the rest of it six parts whitewash to four parts pebble dash. No Little Chef this.

Mine wasn't the only saloon car parked there but I still felt like a fart in a spacesuit. Unwelcome.

In we went nonetheless. The door making that electronic two-tone 'beep boop' noise as it opened and again as it slowly slid shut. If I worked in somewhere with one of those I'd go mental. We got coffees and sat facing the front with them. They were doing Sunday lunches, which I thought was novel, but I chose not to partake. If the only aroma you can discern is gravy, then it's not worth it.

Shortly, a shiny red Volvo rig, minus its trailer, rolled into the car park, air-brakes hissing. Extra halogens adorning it like jewellery and some sort of bull-bar affair that looked like a flattened hockey net stuck out from the grill like a Hannibal Lecter mask. Jennifer indicated that this was our man.

"He's called Smudge," she informed me.

The name didn't suit him one bit I thought, as he lumbered out of the cab. Too cute for a start. Blob, or Orca, or Jabba maybe. You get the idea.

He wobbled in through the door, which did its irritating noise again. Twice. He got nods from some of the other truckers, but warm welcomes didn't seem to be on the menu.

"Who's this?" he said as he flopped down on a chair across the table from us, jabbing a finger the size and shape of a magic marker in my general direction. Without actually looking directly at me. His eyes were the proverbial piss holes in the snow.

"He's my boyfriend," said Jen. Resting her head on my shoulder. We hadn't discussed anything of the sort. Shut down a few avenues of negotiation from the start.

"You stupid bitch." He stared at her. "He's no business here." I was still getting no eye contact from Smudge. He turned away to look at the chalkboard menu on the wall.

"Actually, I'm from the Royal Mail," I said. "We'd heard

113

about the size of your arse and I'm here to assign it its very own postcode."

He finally looked at me. I think his nostrils flared but - he had that much face - I couldn't swear to it. I thought I'd best just get on with it.

"Tell me: Who's the guy with the Aston Martin."

Couldn't get simpler than that, could it?

"You know what you can do mate? You can fuck right off!" he spat.

He pushed his face towards me but as he did so my left hand whipped out and straight back again, chopping him quickly in the front of his fat neck with the edge of my palm. Both hands were wrapped back around my coffee mug and I was sat there, the picture of innocence, before he even had time to register the pain. When he did, his eyes rolled back briefly and he started making a sound not dissimilar to an asthmatic terrier. His hands gripped the edge of the formica table, knuckles turning white. Jen gasped a sharp intake of breath and gripped my knee under the table. I wasn't happy about it but said nowt, focusing everything on the tough guy act for the time being.

A few people glanced over at the noise. I shrugged and smiled.

"Bad brussel sprout. He'll be fine."

Then I leaned in a little closer to him, hushed my voice, but kept the tone and my mannerisms conversational. Under the table I quietly removed Jen's hand from my leg, where it had slid a little further up.

"In a couple of minutes, Smudge, you will regain the use of your vocal cords. When you do, please be a good boy and answer my question."

Whilst he sat there with his eyes watering, making little involuntary swallows, I explained to him that Jennifer would no longer be coming to him for her gear and that, if she ever heard from him again, the consequences would involve more physical pain, damage to his beloved rig and a

114

visit from my mates on the drug squad. All in the style of a friendly chat.

Finally, he managed to make a rasping reply.

"His name is Greg." Cough.

"Surname?"

"D'ancona." Swallow.

"You his dealer?"

He paused and then shook his head. I could see that a kind of mental double-take had gone on inside him. My impression was that, if such a relationship existed, it was the other way round. The guy with the silly name might well be his supplier.

"Where do I find him?"

"I don't know where he lives." Gulp. "But he'll find you." Wheeze. "And you'll be sorry you asked." Retch.

At that we got up and left, Jen tugging at my arm as we exited the café, our departure heralded by further electronic cacophony.

"God, he looked like he was about to throw up!" She said it like she was impressed.

"That's why we left, babe. It was either him or me. If he started to give me any more B-movie dialogue I don't know how I'd have coped."

I had a bit of a heart flutter, the way you do after confrontations, could feel it clicking in my throat, but it was the kind you could hide from the outside world and would soon be gone.

"I loved the way you handled him. Ever thought of becoming a headmaster?"

"Not at your school. Girls scare the bejaysus out of me."

"I'd never have guessed."

"Deception is the better part of valour."

We got into the car. I buckled up, but she neglected to.

"What if he does bother me again? Will you do all the things you said you would?" she asked somewhat breathlessly. Maybe the walk across the car park had been too much for her.

"Naa, those were idle threats."

"You're not interested in defending my honour then?"

I sighed.

"Jen, we just met. Maybe you've helped me with what I'm working on, maybe you haven't. I'm busy right now. My friend's daughter, your pupil, is missing. If you want to hire me in the future to build a criminal case against the guy then we'll see, but by then the damage would be done. I don't hire on to do revenge work and I really do have other things to do. Sorry." My voice sounded tired to me.

It was her turn to sigh. Then she slid down a little in the seat and swivelled her knees towards me. Her skirt rose up a little as she did so.

"Would you blackmail me to get me into bed?"

I was checking the rear view to see whether a gang of truckers might be descending on us but I could just catch the batting of her eyelashes in my peripheral vision. Those were some lashes, as I've said, but even they were beginning to annoy me.

"Perhaps I wouldn't go quite as far as blackmail..." I turned to her.

"You wouldn't have to..."

Oh for fuck's sake.

"Put your seat belt on," I snapped. Turned the ignition on, put the car into gear and almost fish-tailed out onto the main road.

"Where to?"

Silence. She had her arms folded across her chest and was staring resolutely out of the window. After a couple of minutes driving I spoke again.

"In the absence of any instructions from you, I'll just drop you off at the pub where I picked you up. Yeah?"

More silence. You'd think I'd chopped *her* in the throat.

We got there and I dropped her off in the car park. I started to say thank you, goodbye and all that, but she just stormed off into the pub.

116

Once back on the road my mobile vibrated with a message from her. I pressed hot key to read it.

It just said: COCKMASTER!

I had to pull over I was laughing that hard.

I turned tail and headed back to the pub. She was sat in there with a face like a wet weekend so I got the beers in and went and sat at the table with her. We remained in silence, inches from each other yet communicating purely by text until the smiling built up and laughter eventually overtook us both. She dropped the femme fatale act and I removed me head from up me arse and we got on just fine after that. Life's too short.

Chapter 18

Greg D'ancona. What kind of a name was that? Probably not the kind that Smudge would have come up with straight off as a lie, under duress. It was encouraging. Tracking someone down by his or her surname is easier if it's an odd one.

'You'll be sorry you asked.' The suggestion there that this Greg was someone heavy. Someone you wouldn't want to mess with. An unsavoury character. Not exactly a suitable life partner for Trevini's daughter. See you soon, Greg.

By now the police should have followed up the lead from Daphne and Co. I should go and see how cooperative they really were. After lunch with Jen that was. I went for the mixed grill rather than the roast dinner. I was on to pints now. I had a Badger Original followed by a Tanglefoot. Both local brews. I slightly favoured the latter, but there wasn't much in it. Jennifer moved on to a Riesling. Casting my mind back to last Sunday in the Old Dolphin with Kelp I felt a pang of guilt. I've served up enough hospital food in my time to know that Sunday dinners were the absolute worst. He'd be suffering from more than physical pain right now, that's if he was even onto solids yet. I owed him big style when he got out.

So I turned up at the station. It was a relatively new building on the outskirts of town. I introduced myself and asked for the PC who I'd spoken to yesterday by his collar number, which I'd committed to memory. If he'd been working Saturday he was probably working Sunday too.

He wasn't there, but the desk sergeant had been brought up to speed and invited me through. He was a friendly looking chap with greying hair and a moustache. We sat in a little side room with the door propped open so he could see if anyone came to the desk. There was also a window through which you could see anyone coming up the steps outside.

The gist of what he told me was that Francesca Trevini appeared to have left the school of her own free will and, distressing though it must be for her father, the best thing to do for the present time was just to wait and see. Kids that age etc, statistics have shown us, blah blah.

"Have you followed up the lead on the car? Quite a distinctive model," I said.

"We have spoken to a gentleman who owns such a vehicle. He does indeed remember giving a lift to a schoolgirl, whilst on his way home, some time ago. I'm afraid he can't help us any further than that."

"On his way home? That would mean he lives out somewhere beyond the school, then."

"It's irrelevant where he lives."

"No it's not. If he lives in completely the opposite direction from Blandford then he's lying."

"It's irrelevant to *you*. We are not helping you in *your* investigation. You may be of some help to *us* in ours. If so, we can cooperate."

"Yeah? How do you see that happening?"

"If it happens that we bring anyone in for questioning then your personal knowledge of Miss Trevini may be useful to us."

"*If?* So you haven't bought this guy in for questioning then?"

"We have contacted him."

"What's that supposed to mean? You've phoned him?"

"This particular line of enquiry is going nowhere. We have spoken to the gentleman concerned and are not questioning him any further."

"Could I use your phone please? Something has just occurred to me."

He made a 'be my guest' gesture and I went and used the phone positioned under the front desk. I phoned the school and spoke to the receptionist. The sergeant came and stood in the doorway and listened to the questions I was asking. He seemed to pick up on what I was doing and started to get a little irritated, shifting from one foot to the other, waiting for me to finish. Afterwards, we went back through to the little room.

"Right," I started. "As you ought to know, the reception at the school keeps a record of times that pupils sign in and out. From what I can ascertain, and I'd probably need to speak to Francesca's room-mates again to be absolutely sure, on the day that this 'lift' looks like having occurred - "

"Looks like?" he interjected. I just continued:

" - Francesca's three room-mates arrived back, en masse, over two hours before she did. Francesca left town before they did, in an Aston Martin. How do they beat her back to base? By two hours? Yer man is lying."

"Not necessarily. He may have dropped her off, and she may have chosen to walk around for a while before signing back in."

"Sergeant. Please tell me what is so special about Greg D'ancona that you seem to be going out of your way to protect him?"

That threw him for a second. I thought he might chuck me out there and then but he took a deep breath and actually seemed to relax a little.

"Very good, Mr. O'Brien. I'm impressed."

"Just watch me. By tonight I'll have his address."

"Not from me you won't. And I advise you not to harass him in any way."

"I'm only going to question him. I'll be nice."

"He has already been questioned by us Mr. O'Brien. We are the professionals."

"Oh that's alright then. I'll just go home, shall I? I'm sorry but you are not filling me with confidence right now."

"Mr. D'ancona is a very powerful man with very powerful lawyers."

He was leaning in towards me, voice almost hushed, softening, trying to bring me round to his way of thinking.

"Oh? Been in trouble before has he? Lawyers strike me as more your problem than mine. I couldn't give a shit."

He sighed. "Mr. D'ancona has no criminal record."

"Not for the want of trying?"

He shrugged. "O'Brien." He'd dropped the Mr. and I could sense where this was going – man to man, off the record, take my advice, that sort of thing. He continued:

"We have all sort of things going on down here. Try not to think of us as some sleepy village with bobbies on push-bikes."

"The image hadn't even entered my mind."

"We have organized crime, like you have in the cities: drugs, prostitution. We also have problems particular to our locale. Untaxed tobacco and alcohol coming in off the coast; hundreds of anonymous cattle sheds and barns for storing contraband and for staging dog fights and bare knuckle box-ing matches; then there's Red Diesel…"

"Crop circles? Big Cat sightings?"

Entertaining as his 'we're not just a one horse town' speech was, I was getting impatient. He just rambled on though. "And organized crime has powerful people behind it. People who organize it."

"You're talking Mr. Big; Overlord; *Capo de tutti capo*; Criminal mastermind; Evil Genius hellbent on World Domination…That kind of thing?"

He paused and shook his head. Gave me the look that he probably reserved for cocky suspects who were spending far too long in the interview room.

"You quite fancy yourself, don't you, O'Brien?"

"I try not to fly in the face of public opinion."

He shook his head again.

"Well," he continued, "if there was such an 'Organizer', don't you think he'd have a bunch of high priced lawyers ready to protect his backside?"

"So you're suggesting…"

He held a hand up to stop me.

"I'm not suggesting anything at all. That would certainly not be in my best interests."

"Damn those lawyers. But like I said - "

"Quite. You 'couldn't give a shit'. How admirable. But such a person would not only have lawyers to protect himself, would he?"

"Yeah, I get it. Evil henchmen; Goons; Enforcers. That kind of thing?"

I felt like adding 'bent coppers' but stopped just short.

"So you follow me?" He smiled at me, like we were finally getting somewhere.

"Message received and understood," I said.

"I hope you do understand. This is a friendly warning not to bite off more than you can chew."

"Okay. Thank you. But a young girl is missing. Her disappearance appears to be linked to someone who you are 'not suggesting' is suspected of all sorts of dodgy goings-on that he's too clever to have pinned on him. Meanwhile, back on my manor, there's been a murder; arson with intent to endanger life; attempted murder - all seemingly centring around my client who happens to be the father of the missing girl. Well, excuse me, but I don't like it. And that means I'm going to do something about it and - as far as I'm concerned - you can stick your friendly warning, because your friendly warning, plus a quid, will buy me a cup of coffee."

At that he pushed himself up from his seat, his body stiffening, his attitude formal once more.

"Is that your car outside, Mr. O'Brien?" He nodded towards the window. My Escort was across the road and I don't know if he really looked. I just replied that it was.

"And is that beer that I can smell on your breath?"

Busted.

"I just had the one at lunch," I lied.

"Well, I suggest that you put some thought into not overdoing it. In any sense of the word. Wouldn't want to fall foul of the law whilst you were down here, would you?"

I had been pushing it somewhat and I realised it. The guy was probably just trying to help in his own little limited way. The worst of it was that Jennifer had given me a teenth of draw as a goodbye present and I'd totally forgotten that it was nestling in my shirt pocket as I sat there. What an eejit. Suddenly all I wanted to do was get out of there.

I stood up too, throwing my hands up in a surrendering gesture and he kindly showed me to the door. I walked across to my car, in a straight line, and got in. I didn't look back to see if he was watching me but I buckled up, checked the rear view, checked the blind spot, all that shit, before indicating out into traffic and driving at exactly 30mph back to the hotel.

If I imagined hard enough, I could pretend Debra was there waiting for me. She would take me in her arms and tell me everything was going to be okay.

Chapter 19

No, Debra wasn't there waiting. The pillows weren't even in the same huggable position I'd left them in that morning. The Devil take those chambermaids.

I took a shower. Showers are almost recreational to me and it helped sober me up a bit too, not that it mattered. I had every intention of getting tanked later on.

Then I headed out for a stroll. Passing by the watermeadows and pausing on the bridge, staring down into the dark waters of the river Stour as if it held all the answers. If it did they were not apparent to me and I strolled on. Eventually I found a proper quaint little tobacconists that sold pipes ranging from the inexpensive, through the ineffective (that's clay pipes for you), to the quite frankly ridiculous. I told you I smoke like a girl? Yeah, well I roll like a spastic. I bought a bog standard pipe, a quarter ounce of black cherry tobacco, a lighter, and made my furtive way back to the hotel.

Chris O'Brien - Dope Fiend

So there I was, sat on the bed, burning and crumbling tiny fragments of the small block of resin into the moist contents of the pipe. I sparked up and thought - if my mates could see me now. I must have looked a complete donkey.

It was over a year since I'd last touched the stuff and, yep, it was every bit as mediocre as I remembered from then.

Time to phone Trevini and bring him up to date again. It was hard to know what to tell him without making it sound bad. I emphasized the fact that I thought Fran was safe, that she wasn't being held against her will, but we agreed that there was a worrying side to the possible 'boyfriend'. His voice was wavering close to tears at times but he kept saying how grateful he was that I was down here, that he was sure I would find her. I wanted to tell him not to have too much confidence in me, but how the hell are you supposed to say something like that? It wasn't as if I was holding his pool cue whilst he went to the toilet.

I asked if there had been any further incidents up there and he said no. He gathered himself a little and asked if I wanted him to send anyone down to assist me. Thanks but no thanks. An army of doormen and pasta chefs wasn't necessarily going to yield any faster results. Perhaps he could send Evie. She could cook me deep-fried Camembert with cranberry sauce whilst I detected. Just a thought. A stoned thought?

What I did ask though was for him to contact an acquaintance of his and ask her to ring me. He was only too happy to oblige. She contacted me within twenty minutes on my mobile. I preferred her doing that than ringing the hotel in case any of the Dorset criminal fraternity were listening in on me. Dope paranoia?

"Chris, hello darling! Lorenzo has been telling me all about it. Poor Francesca. I'm at your disposal, obviously, but how do you think I can help?"

Her name was Paula Prescatta. I'd met her at one of Trevini's gatherings and she was what you might refer to as a 'socialite'. She was involved, 'very very loosely' she'd told me, in Operatic productions. She wrote something occasionally in some high-class rag and she went to a hell of a lot of parties. By her own admission, she knew *everyone*.

In the surreal mood that I found myself in, I figured that I couldn't go wrong.

"Hi Paula. Thank you for calling. Do you know someone called Greg D'ancona?"

I went on to give her the secondhand physical description, told her about the car he drove and the level of wealth implied, that he appeared to live in Dorset, the suggestion that he may be involved with drugs. When I said that he may also have property in Chelsea she replied "Who doesn't?". As far as she was concerned, the above information applied to most of the young men of her acquaintance but the name

D'ancona did ring a bell. She would make some calls and get back to me. In the social circles she moved in it was apparently quite the norm to conduct in-depth research on one's peers. Fame or charisma could get you a long way but, other than that, the right background was essential in order to be in with the in-crowd. Her manner was such that I had total confidence in her ability to find out who this floppy haired freak was.

I headed down to the bar. I was back on the lager, again doing that little self delusion, telling myself it would keep my head clearer than if I was drinking bitter. They didn't have any Rock so I was about to settle for Becks when I saw some Dos Equis tucked away in the chill cabinet.

Ahh, *cervesa*.

There was a dish of roasted almonds on the bar top and I got stuck into them. *Ski Sunday* was on the box and two middle-aged gents in garish Fred Perry turtlenecks were holding their stomachs in and having a conversation, just slightly too loudly, about their exploits in Aiguille du Midi, Chamonix. An impressively large chalkboard, which had a frame worthy of an oil painting, announced an extensive evening menu. They must have used special hi-tech chalk to write that small and neat. In thicker, more permanent lettering at the bottom we were told that Christmas Day was fully booked. I took a couple more unopened bottles back up to my room. I deliberately tried to drink really slowly, just sipping at the bottle whilst doing some leg-stretching exercises on the floor. I soon gave that a miss. I was halfway down the second bottle and was loading up another pipe, sat on the bed in just my Calvin Kleins with the telly on, when Paula phoned back.

"Chris. I've researched Gregory D'ancona for you and this is what I have found. Are you going to take this down? Have you got a pen and paper at hand?"

I hadn't thought of that but it sounded like a good idea, in case I woke up tomorrow and thought it was all a dream. I asked her to hang on whilst I turned the sound down on the TV, scrabbled around and found something suitable.

"Paula. Sorry about that. Go ahead."

"Now, here we are. The first bit's courtesy of my dear friend Prof. Stott and it's a bit of a history lesson really. Quite a story."

"Go for it. I'm a sucker for a bit of history. I've got *Time Team* on with the sound down." It was true.

"Oh, Tony Robinson? He's a darling! Anyway, the D'anconas have been over here since the Normandy Landing."

I suspected she meant the Norman Conquest but I let it ride. She was supposed to be better educated than me. She continued, "They amassed quite a fortune over the years in farming and shipping. Their wealth plateaued a few hundred years ago. The lucrative shipping moved away from the Dorset coast and the farming profited consistently but with no growth."

Sounded like she was reading from some notes she'd made.

"The D'anconas never really made it into the industrial revolution, invested badly when they did. Their wealth continued to dwindle over the last century, with farming taking a real downturn from the late 60s onwards. Yet still coping, bringing in just enough to run the big old family home. Until the late 80s, that was. Black Monday and all that."

"The stock market crash. I even remember the date. 19th October 1987." I remember it because it had kicked the shit out of my uncle and the small business he was building at the time.

"Exactly. Family facing complete ruin. Within two months, Desmond and Rosemary D'ancona had taken their own lives, leaving their only son an orphan, a week from Christmas. Gregory D'ancona was just fourteen years old. Heir to whatever was left, which wasn't much."

"And that's our man Greg? Mid to late twenties now?"

127

"Twenty-seven. And do you know what he did? This is the impressive part, Chris; he built the family fortune – his fortune now – back to its former glory."

"How so?"

"The death of his parents freed up a trust fund that allowed him to pay for a private education and, whilst still a schoolboy, he began to invest in both computer software and communications technology, which were growing at the time."

"Still are."

"Exactly. Remember those days? One fax machine to a whole office building if you were lucky, or an attic room full of telex equipment if you weren't. Mobile phones the size of a handbag? Well, he was in on the ground floor. Made a killing in property too."

Paula was obviously more at home with this end of the story than the historical beginnings.

"Tell me more."

"Well, I asked round a number of people in the know. Greg was top of his classes at Bryanston, just across the road from you, darling. Spent two years on a friend's father's rubber plantation in Malaysia, doing lord knows what except playing the market from afar, before going up to Cambridge to obtain a first in Psychology followed by an MBA. Since then he's just invested. He owns countless properties and businesses across the Home Counties. He's acquiring new ones all the time, according to a star-struck acquaintance of mine. He is estimated to be worth around £55 million."

"Excuse me one moment Paula... Okay, I'm back. Carry on."

"What was that?"

"That was just me picking myself back up off the floor."

"Oh you! But his real wealth isn't easy to assess and apparently he's not that forthcoming about it, so he's never made the *Sunday Times Rich List*."

"Is Trevini a millionaire?" It had never occurred to me but now I was interested.

"Chris! Lorenzo is valued at around £8 million. Is he a millionaire? A million is positively nothing these days."

"You don't say. So, apart from fast cars, what are Greg's interests?"

"Hmm, does all the usual – hunting; shooting; riding; skiing. Apparently he boxed for Cambridge. But here's where it gets somewhat esoteric. I'm reading this off a fax so I don't know if my pronunciation's correct but neither do I care. He has studied – *Pentjak Silat*?"

"It's an Indonesian martial art. I've never seen it in action. He'll have picked that up in Malaysia."

"And holds a fourth Dan black belt in – *Tang Soo Do*?"

"That's Korean. Lots of kicking."

"My source has written 'allegedly' in such big letters in front of the next bit and made it quite clear that his name is never to be mentioned in connection with what I am about to tell you."

"Soul of discretion. Go on."

"There is talk that he is involved in those barbaric unlicensed boxing matches, you know the things…"

"Bare knuckle, anything goes?"

"Indeed. And, which is even more startling for an educated gentleman, he is rumoured to enjoy taking part in the actual fighting."

Yeah, I could just see him. Poncing about in his Jacques Tatte trousers with his hair tied back, dancing round some hairy-arsed gypsy fella who's too scared to hit him because he's the Guvnor.

"He likes to party," she continued.

"Who doesn't?"

"He's single and he's not gay."

"Pity. I was beginning to quite fancy him," I lied. More like intense loathing, despite any sympathy I might have had for his 'traumatic' childhood.

"You wouldn't be the only one. Very popular with the debutante set. The rumour is that if you're over eighteen he won't even look at you."

"That's me out on two counts then." But Francesca definitely in.

"And really, that's about all I can tell."

"Paula, you are a marvel."

"It has been really quite fascinating. Don't you just love these stories of triumph over adversity? Who was it who said 'that which doesn't kill us, makes us stronger'?"

"That was Friedrich Nietzsche." I don't think she'd actually expected the answer.

"Oh, well it does sound a very German thing to say."

He was Austrian, but I thought it politic to leave it at that.

"It's more than I could have hoped for, Paula, but I don't suppose you have an address?"

"If I did it would be one of many. But he does base himself in Dorset, very large residence, somewhere secluded."

"Okay. Lets 'do lunch' in the big city when all this is over. My treat."

"Dear sweet Chris. You and I both know you can't afford me."

"Your treat then."

"Done."

With that she was gone. I sat there feeling a little the wiser but wondering where it was going to get me. I stared down at my empty bottle. Well, that was one problem which could be easily addressed.

Earlier in the day I had told that policeman that I would have D'ancona's address by now and it pissed me off that I hadn't. It might not seem like much but I have a belief that each time someone makes a promise they fail to keep, they lose a part of themselves.

I got dressed again and headed down to the bar. I had promised myself more beer and I was going to make damn sure I stuck to that one.

Chapter 20

I left it until well after midnight to phone that number in Chelsea, hoping to catch someone off guard; defenses down; no cover story at the ready. Anyway, it just rang and rang. No answer.

I dialled 192. I told them Dorset. I said it was probably something Hall, or Mansions, or Palace. I told them the name was D'ancona. They told me they had nothing listed for that. I think they wanted to tell me something else but politeness prevented them.

Monday morning I tried the Chelsea number again. Nada. I put on some sweats and my Reeboks and managed a run before breakfast. I headed over the river, through the gatehouse and into the grounds of Bryanston.

It was a muddy, trudging affair through an audience of naked trees, but that's how all my runs had been over the past couple of months. *When yellow leaves, or none, or few do hang upon those boughs that shake against the cold. Bare ruined choirs where late the sweet birds sang.* Even a bit of snow would have been welcome. As I worked up a reasonable cadence I began to imagine, with each footfall, that a young and uncorrupted D'ancona may have trod where I had trod. That didn't last long because soon my head was full of 'We Gotta Get Out of this Place' by The Animals. It's pretty much my running mantra. Maybe it would have stayed in my head all day, which would have been fine with me, if some moron hadn't been pumping out Britney Spears' latest when I got back to the hotel.

After breakfast I headed to the library and searched records from local papers around the time of the D'ancona suicide. Benzodiazepine and paracetamol overdose the pair of them. They had apparently waited until young Gregory was away on a local camping trip. She was found dead in

131

bed upstairs. He was collapsed on the kitchen floor. All deeply tragic.

Suicide has long been statically high amongst the farming community, partly due to economic pressures and the culture of staunch independence that makes it difficult to ask for help. But mainly because they are so damn good at it compared to the general public. This is to do with their access to firearms. Farmers are more likely to shoot themselves than overdose. Ask any psych nurse and they'll tell you that overdosing is a very hit and miss way of ending it all. Shooting yourself is not. Still, maybe they were just trying to make it less traumatic for the son they were leaving behind.

The articles provided no clues as to where D'ancona might be living now so I browsed thoroughly through all the available maps before heading to the Tourist Info and buying the most relevant ones. My plan was to basically work outwards from Blandford, concentrating first on the line out past Fran's school, looking for large habitations. The key word that I held in my head was "secluded". It wasn't going to be in the middle of a bunch of houses, and maybe it wasn't going to be somewhere you could easily see from a main road.

After two hours of driving I had crossed a few possibles off the map, but I was also beginning to baulk at the enormity of my task. I was getting nowhere fast.

But I was being followed.

It was not an Aston Martin. It was a heap of shit old model Nissan Micra, in white. It wasn't doing too bad. Staying at least two cars behind when it could, not there all the time. But after two hours it was beyond a joke. I must have made a difficult target in that I had no destination. My movements probably would have appeared random and erratic to my tail. They would have done better to give up early on and not risk exposure in that situation but that Micra kept turning up like a bad penny.

The easiest thing to do if you're being tailed is just to pull over. They'll either go sailing past and that's that or they'll park up too and you've got a Mexican standoff. The other thing is to try and lose them. If your pursuer wishes to stay discreet then it's pretty easy to do. If they want to stay with you at all costs then that's where your actual car chase comes in. Never done one.

What I wanted to do here was different. I wanted to catch the person who was following me, in the sense of actually getting my hands on him. That meant trapping him. Boxing him in somewhere so he had nowhere to run to, nowhere to hide.

For that I needed a dead end. Preferably not somewhere residential but I wasn't choosy right now. I remembered a cul-de-sac I'd seen on the Saturday afternoon and headed for the area, driving just like I was just on my way home from work. As we approached my target along a long residential street, the traffic thinned out so that there were no cars between me and my pursuer. He still hung well back, though.

Just as I approached the turning I let my speed creep up a little before throwing the car round to the left and up the cul-de-sac. A real pro tailer would have crept round the turning behind me, or even cruised past and rerouted later. This guy did the amateur thing of speeding as soon as I'd got out of sight so as not to lose me.

This had the effect that he whipped round into the street too fast and sailed past me where I'd immediately pulled up on the left. As soon he registered that there was just a stretch of empty road with houses at the end, I was back out behind him blocking his exit. Let's rock.

I almost rear-ended the Micra as I forced it up to the small turning circle at the top. At the last minute I slewed the Escort across the road just to make sure. I killed the engine and leapt out.

Suddenly I knew exactly what that 'red mist' was that everyone talks about. I'm normally an easy-going kind of guy but everything that had been going on over the past week and a half, everything that had left me feeling so powerless, everything that had seen me displace my frustration onto convenient authority figures – policemen; security guards...even schoolteachers for crissakes. It had all come to a head. And this fucker was going to cop for it.

I stormed over to the driver's side and yanked the door open without a thought for the danger I might be facing.

"Right! I'm gonna fuc - " But I froze. Body and mind.

Sat staring up at me was Debra Prentice.

I couldn't believe it. She smiled and spoke:

"Hello China. Now don't be lettin' your mouth write cheques your ass can't cash."

She started to climb out of the vehicle. I almost had to instruct my body to move out of her way. It was like the first time we had met. Except the air was full of a different kind of electricity.

"What the FUCK do you think YOU are doing here!!!?" I yelled, finally managing to make a sound and more than making up for my momentary silence. I don't think I've ever shouted like that. It came up from my boots and it honestly scared me.

Around us, curtains were twitching. So were the veins in my temples.

Debra, however, leaned lazily against the chassis of her car and looked at me like I'd just asked her if she wanted a cuppa.

"Free country," she shrugged.

I lost it then. The energy had to go somewhere and I just started flapping my arms about and literally jumping up and down. I was babbling and ranting. Just stream of consciousness insults and accusations. Stuff about she should be at her brother's side; people were dying and she didn't care; there might even have been some bizarre shit about being an unfit mother. I don't know. I do remember what I topped it all off with, though:

"Just FUCK OFF and LEAVE ME ALONE!"

She just looked at me this time. Still relaxed but with her arms folded across her chest and something a little harder in her eyes.

"You finished?" she asked.

"I don't know," I said petulantly. Beginning to deflate.

"Give you another couple of minutes if you want?"

"Debra, why on earth are you here?"

"Kel's healing nicely. He's fine. I'm not fine. I'm pissed off."

Funny. She didn't really look it. She continued, "He told me what you said about his assailants probably being from Dorset…"

Assailants. Hark at her.

"So I came to Dorset. See what I could see."

"And ended up following me? To see if you could see what I was seeing?"

She spread her hands.

"I'm sorry. I didn't mean to get spotted. This detecting business isn't as easy as you make it look."

I had to smile at that.

"Actually, babe, you were a damn good tail. You just happened to be following me is all."

She smiled at that one.

"Well, aren't we just slicker than goose shit?"

We low-fived, as if it was something we'd done a thousand times, and then hugged for about a minute. People were coming out onto their doorsteps now and watching us. Now that they could see no one was being murdered. Maybe interracial hugs were a hanging offence, though.

"Where you staying?" I asked.

She cocked her head backwards towards the Micra.

"You're sleeping in the car?"

"I've got a tent in the back."

"Oh, that's much more sensible. Can I just remind you it's December?"

She shrugged and said, "That which doesn't kill you..."

"Makes you stronger. Yeah, so I've heard. Did you know Nietzsche died of pneumonia?"

"Nietzsche was a big girl's blouse."

This girl just absolutely cracked me up. I hugged her again. When I'd finished I said, "Come stay at the hotel."

"No." So decisive. "Me being around you right now is only going to amplify your insecurities. Make you less effective. Don't want you worrying about protecting me."

"It's going to *what* my *what*?"

"We can cover more ground separately. You can even tell me what to do, where to go. You've got the detecting experience. If you don't want that – fine. Forget that I'm here. I'm not your concern. I'll find my own leads or give up and go home. But I'm not sleeping with you. " She paused. "I also strongly suggest you don't sleep with anyone else."

"What are you now? My manager?"

I wondered then if she'd followed me and Jennifer. No. Not in that car she hadn't.

"Look. Let's move our cars so that these good people can get back to their lives. Let's go eat something and, if you want, you can tell me everything you know."

"That sounds great. We'll go eat at Terra Firma in Shaftesbury. There's nowt in Blandford."

"How do I get there?" she said as we both were getting into our respective vehicles.

"Follow me," I replied.

She laughed.

"Christ, O'Brien. Make up your goddamn mind!"

Chapter 21

It was quite a drive but it was worth it. I had a warm salad with chorizo sausage and avocado. Debra had one with tofu and tiny shreds of oyster mushroom. Between us we had a big bowl of cous cous, overflowing with multicolored peppers and courgettes, and a small dish of aioli which Debra didn't touch - I guess because of the egg white. I drank a bottle of Tusker, African beer and she had spring water.

"Did you guess I was vegan?" she asked.

"I thought at least you'd be vegetarian. You can't eat red meat and be as relaxed as you are. Anyway, I'm looking forward to cooking for you now. Some of my most creative dishes are vegan."

"Don't drink or smoke either," she said.

"Oh. And I was really looking forward to getting pissed with you."

"You still can."

"Have you any vices whatsoever?" I enquired.

"I love coffee. Too much. I plan to give it up by the time I'm thirty."

She said it like she really meant it.

So we talked. First I wanted to know as much as possible about how Kelp was doing. He wasn't mobile yet and still needed an operation on his knee. He was in good spirits but still got a lot of internal pain when he moved around in the bed. Combination of ruptured spleen, broken ribs and torn intercostals.

Then I told her everything I'd learnt. She was silent for the most part but she whispered "Slapper," when I told her about Jennifer Culliver. She mouthed "Wow" when I told her about D'ancona's wealth, and she sucked a little air through her teeth when I mentioned his martial arts pretensions.

We decided that it would be best if we took half the map

each and just carried on the same reconnaissance that I'd been doing. I wasn't looking forward to it. I wanted to stay here all day. The rain was back. Lashing the windows and turning the Shaftesbury cobblestones slick and black. We traded mobile numbers and said we would contact each other if we saw any likely suspects.

Over espressos, we lapsed into a comfortable silence. As comfortable as if she'd been a male friend. After a while though she looked at me and said, "Nietzsche didn't die of pneumonia."

That threw me, but I answered, "No. He died from complications of..."

"Syphilis." She finished my sentence for me.

"Yeah. I was just trying to be clever."

"Well that's your problem. You just are. So don't try to be."

"Hey who's supposed to be the *Daoist* here? Me or you?"

She shrugged. "Did you hear what the Daoist monk said to the hot dog vendor?"

"No."

"Make me One with Everything."

And that's when I told her that I was completely head over heels in love with her. That I knew I would never want anyone else the way I wanted her. That I wanted to be by her side always and forever.

I didn't tell her it out loud though. Didn't want her thinking I was insecure and, anyway, if she was as good as I thought she was she'd have read my mind.

Chapter 22

It would have been better to just stay there and study the maps, I thought, as the windscreen wipers waged war against the onslaught of rain. Could hardly make out oncoming traffic, let alone the features of the landscape.

In the next three hours I only managed to cross off two 'possibles'. It wasn't the best time of year either, dark by half past four. At least Debra was here now, cutting down the workload. I didn't doubt her decision making for one second. If it had been her brother then I'd have to retrace his steps for myself, making it pointless to even enlist help in the first place. We contacted each other by phone a couple of times to say which area we were eliminating but I had to drive a little way to get a signal at one point.

We met up at the hotel and worked on the maps until late. There were a couple of fancy vegan choices on the menu downstairs but Debra was happy with two bowls of vegetable soup and a ton of bread rolls.

We lay together on the bed, belly down, with the maps spread out. You couldn't have slotted a sheet of paper between us and it felt so good.

But when the time came she got up to leave. I was incredulous.

"Are you really going to go put a tent up in the dark? In the wet? In the cold?"

"Come watch me if you don't believe."

So she went. Just as the door was closing I shouted after her:

"Debra!"

"China?"

"You try too hard, too."

She smiled but, for the first time, there was a hint of weakness and self doubt to it.

"I told you we were alike."

And she was gone.

Tuesday morning. I phoned both Tim and Trevini to try and make reassuring noises. Tim sounded real distant. When I spoke to Trevini he confirmed that he'd ordered Tim off work and the doctor had given him something. Trevini had thought I'd probably ask so he'd memorised it. Lorazepam and Zopiclone. A muscle relaxant and a sleeper. Tim had said nowt.

I phoned Debra and just confirmed the tasks we'd set for ourselves the previous night. I got the impression that the phone call was a waste of time. We both knew what we were doing and she wasn't the kind of person who went "No, you hang up first, no, you first!" We weren't meeting for lunch but we'd get together again at the end of the day unless anything cropped up before then. Her phone had been on charge at the hotel the previous evening in preparation for today.

Visibility was better than yesterday. Everywhere there was a constant drizzle that seemed to float. It was more like a mood of the sky than a meteorological phenomena. Elemental emotion.

Late morning I was up on a place called Hod Hill. I remembered from yesterday at the Tourist Info that it had been the site of a hill fort in the Iron Age and later a Roman cavalry position. It was part of Cranbourne Chase, a large area of rolling hills, woodland and grazing land that stretched all the way to Wiltshire in the east. The whole area was a traditional hunting ground. Yes, the irony struck me. But not as much as it did later.

I couldn't see down into the valley, but that was kind of promising in itself. It warranted investigation. I started driving tentatively down a number of tracks – some forestry commission, some farms. They just led to hay deposits or logging sites except for one.

It seemed to go on and on but was just getting rougher

and muddier. The Escort wasn't going to make it any further so I got out. It was time to have a look over the six-foot brick wall that had been on my left since the bridge over a small stream that divided the land. Though it wasn't a wide stream the banks were real deep, like a proper moat I thought.

Yep, this elaborate wall wasn't here to keep farm animals from roaming.

I upped and over, dropping down into dense deciduous woodland. The lack of foliage made it easier to navigate, not that I knew where I was going, but the sky was still grey and heavy with drizzle. Off I went, crunching the forest bed underfoot.

It had to have been a mile before it started thinning out and then I could see it. Maybe quarter of a mile down from the trees, across an open field, was a house. Big. Much bigger than Trevini's but still smaller than a girls' boarding school. There was also a wire fence towards the bottom of the field that I estimated to be about nine or ten feet high. Really spoiled the view. Alongside the north of the house was either a set of stables or a garage for a whole collection of cars.

Just at that moment, a section of it rolled up automatically at the front and a four-wheel-drive vehicle came out. I was far enough away to hardly hear the engine but, peering into the open garage from where I was, I thought I could just make out the low-slung rear end of a sports car nestling in there. Dark green. Then the door rolled shut again and it was gone.

It was enough to get me excited, so I tried to phone Debra. Absolutely no signal whatsoever. What can you do?

I headed off back through the same mile of woodland to get my Bins and my trusty Minolta out of the car.

Chapter 23

I made my ascent of the wall quickly and dropped down the other side, in a rush to get my equipment. My mistake. A Mitsubishi Challenger was parked facing my Escort on the opposite side of the track. It was the car that I had seen driving off from the house.

I'd been too excited to check that the coast was clear. To listen out for an engine. Two blokes were sat on the bonnet of my car, waiting for me. If I had had the nouse to come back over the wall in a different location then I might have been able to sneak up on them. As it was I was well and truly trapped.

As if I cared.

I just carried on walking straight towards them. They didn't appear to be armed and I was in a real bad mood.

One of them had sharp weasely features, very dark short hair with a roman fringe. The other was a big lad with a mop of curly hair. They were grinning like idiots, just waiting for me to make my move.

"Captain Troy and Gabriel Oak, I presume?" I said as I approached to within a few feet.

But just as I got the words out there was a flash of something in the wing mirror of the Challenger. Made up for my earlier observational deficits because I had time to jerk my head out and around in reaction. A tyre iron, wielded by a third guy who'd obviously been round the other side of the Challenger, exploded against my cheek.

It had been meant for the middle of my skull, and only the tip of it caught me as it swung on past but it still dropped me down flat in the mud at the feet of the other two guys who started launching kicks at me.

I had to keep moving. I rolled away from them and tried to get up but took one vicious kick on my shoulder that pushed me back down. I wasn't going down flat though. I used the momentum of the fall to roll further away, a proper break fall this time that saw me back on my feet, stumbling wildly. I was in danger of slipping straight back down until there was a moment when my feet found themselves and I seemed to connect to something deep within the earth that pushed me upright.

And then I was running. I like to think the *Dao* picked me up and carried me that day.

They came after me but a gap opened up pretty quick. I was thankful now that I'd had a couple of months of practise in muddy conditions, moving in confident strides. If they were top of the range hard bastards then they probably all smoked forty a day to look the part, another thing in my favour.

The smallest guy was fastest and, when I glanced round and saw that enough of a gap had opened between him and the other two, I let him think he had me.

I slowed, pretended I was flagging; he put on a burst of speed. When I sensed him just behind me I pivoted round and dropped into a horse stance for maximum stability, stuck out my right arm like one wing of an aeroplane and clothes-lined him.

That what you see wrestlers do when one runs full pelt off the ropes and into the extended arm of his opponent. They aim for the top of the sternum to make it look good. I aimed for the throat to make it hurt like hell on toast.

I'd also swung my left arm up to shield my exposed armpit. Never get nutted there because it'll take your nervous system all day to recover. Anyway, it was a clean move. I heard his teeth click together as he connected with my forearm. His feet went from under him and you could almost see him suspended horizontally in midair before he dropped to the floor like a sack of shit.

The other two were still running at me until they skidded to a halt thirty yards shy. It was the fact that I'd stood on their mate's head that halted them. I didn't stomp. I just placed my foot there, but hard, and yelled out:

"He'll die!"

For the first time I started to feel the searing pain in my left cheek, like I had something poisonous and angry growing in there.

And then I did something really stupid. I knew I could out run these two so I should have just legged it but no. I yelled again:

"One down..." And took off running towards them. Vengeance is Mine.

Big Hair turned and ran away, which boosted my confidence further, but the guy who was still holding the tyre iron looked like he wanted some.

He was tall and bony with corded muscle all over, from what you could see of his neck and arms. Bullet-shaped head with cropped sandy hair, big ears, enlarged knuckles - he looked like pain was a way of life to him; exactly what you'd expect a pit-fighter to look like, I suppose.

I stopped short of him and let him swing, staying out of reach and getting the measure of him. I realised I'd made a big mistake. If a guy like this had kicked off in Club Zed then we'd have gone in absolutely mob-handed, no question. Plus he had a weapon, and not something you could block. All I could do was dodge, and I could see his mate - who had run all the way back to the Challenger - was coming back to join in. He appeared to be bringing another blunt object to the party.

To turn my back now would be suicide. He'd just lob the thing at me from a few feet. Fight or die.

I did something I've never done. I thank the adrenaline. A roundhouse kick to the head. Without managing to fall on my arse, either. I took up *Wing Chun* because it's not really a kicking art and I'm not really a kicker but I caught him flush on the ear and knocked him sideways.

When he went sideways I'd landed and was closing the

144

gap to trap his arms when I got my first proper look at the guy running back into the fray. About fifty yards now.

He had a shotgun.

That's when I ran again, taking the chance of a lobbed tyre iron over the alternative. Big ears was back on balance and he was also between me and his mate, in the line of fire. I gave the biggest burst of speed I could without sliding over. Ran past the man who fell to earth. Still out for the count. I remember wishing I'd got a chance to kick him as I went by but also thinking that his mate would hopefully want to run past him too before he risked firing.

That's when I remembered to zig zag, like you read in all those SAS survival books. I also started bearing off to the right, into the sloping tree cover. When I realised that they weren't going to shoot and weren't even running I headed up the hill and into the trees good and proper.

I kept going, running blind now, the fear beginning to really kick in. I was into dense evergreen now and everything darkened. Spruce, fir and holly seemed to close in around me. It was claustrophobic and frightening. Part of my mind started to tell me that there might be more of them, waiting for me.

I couldn't see the road anymore but when I strained I thought I could hear them down there somewhere. They were laughing. Or maybe that was my imagination too.

I kept going, away from where I thought they were, but walking now. It was only after I stopped running that I could feel a stabbing groin strain from having pulled off that kick. I just wanted to move and not to think. That's when the drizzle started to slowly thicken into rain once more until it was pounding and I was soaked to the skin. There was no thunder but the noise of the rain on those trees and shrubs reminded me of electric interference. Ever woken up with a start in your armchair, middle of the night, the bright blankness of the TV screen screeching at you? That moment of confusion when you realise the rest of the world has gone to bed and left you to it? That's how I felt.

Disorientated and alone.

Much, much later I stopped. Allowing myself to think. The SAS manuals would have told me not to walk straight back into the danger area where they could be waiting for me. They'd say "box" around the area and get the hell out of there. If I had to go back to the car then stay well back, set up observation points before making a move. Awareness, Anticipation and Avoidance.

Bollocks.

My clothes were sodden and heavy. My fingers were seizing up and I couldn't feel my feet. I felt like I had a migraine but in my cheekbone rather than my head. I was limping from my groin. The sun hadn't put in an appearance all day and had missed its chance altogether now as the turning of the earth beneath us forced the sky to fag-ash grey and modern lights winked on across an ancient landscape. All I wanted to do was head back to the car and go somewhere dry and warm. If anyone had a problem with that then they could just shoot me.

By the time I got back to the car it was pitch black. Down there below the tree line no lights were visible.

My car had been trashed.

The tyre iron they hadn't had a chance to use on me had seen action after all. There was still a thick acrid smell of burnt plastic and fabric too. It was such a mess. The two bits of good news were that they hadn't found my compartment under the back seat where I keep all my gear, and that the attempt at torching it hadn't caused enough damage to touch it. Turing my Maglite on the scene of destruction I couldn't find any evidence of them having used the shotgun. Perhaps it wasn't loaded. Perhaps they just didn't want to waste ammo or leave it as evidence.

Seeing that it was absolutely undriveable, I had to bite

back the tears. For a brief moment I thanked my lucky stars for Debra before remembering how I couldn't get a signal here before. I checked it again just to be sure. Still nothing. That's when I did start crying.

It was tempting to go and throw myself on D'ancona's mercy. Only a mile or so through woods and fields. All my techno gear in a shoulder bag, not designed to be crammed in there and taken for long walks. I trudged down the track toward civilisation, checking every now and then for a signal, switching the mobile off in between to conserve the battery - even though I could see on the display that it was almost fully charged.

After a mile I was back on a proper road, though not a main one. I hid from every car I heard for fear of it being them. After another mile of walking I got a weak signal. Debra answered on the second ring. I described to her where I was to the best of my knowledge. Probably less than half an hour later - the longest of my life - I saw the white Micra, distinctively rectangular headlights, topping the brow of a low hill two hundred yards to my north. The stars were all out now.

I came out from behind a hedgerow and flagged her down as she approached. Boy was I glad to see a friendly face.

I flopped into the passenger seat and started to tell her everything. I didn't know if I was making sense. She waited until I ran out of words and said: "Perhaps we should have stuck together after all."

I was rallying now, feeling safer. Time for a wisecrack: "No, you'd only have amplified my insecurities."

"Oh shut up!"

"And you might have got shot."

"There is that."

Then I fell asleep. Well, the next thing I remembered was Debra standing outside the passenger door and nudging me.

I couldn't understand how I'd managed to fall to a sleep as the wet chill of my clothes against my skin jerked me to life like a slap from an icy hand. We were in the hotel car park.

"Can you make it up the stairs O.B? Or do I have to carry you?"

"No way. That really would amp- "

"Don't say it," she cut in.

I sat in the shower on full power and heat, trying to shield my cheek from its force. Debra ordered me a simple room service meal. She towelled me off whilst I wolfed a burger that I couldn't taste. The beer, however, was nectar and, unlike me, I never even checked to see which brand it was. My cheek throbbed with every chew and swallow. When I finished, Debra applied a dressing for me.

Then she ordered me onto the bed and started to massage me. I began to warm and loosen. I began to feel the *Qi* flowing through me once more. She whispered to me that she was going to stay.

And we did sleep together that night. Well, we screwed.

It started out as the massage finished, so affectionate at first but turned into a real angry screw which we seemed to both relish and need. I pressed her face down hard into the mattress and growled into her ear all the things I was going to do to her. Describing every dirty deed she could expect from me. And did it all too as she jerked and whimpered. She felt soft and slippery beneath me but I could sense strength surging up from her at times and as soon as there was a lapse in my aggression she had snaked round and was above me. Doing it to me now with more force than any woman I've ever known. Saying things that made me squirm and writhe and want to close my ears for fear of eternal damnation. She was in my brain and knew everything. All the bad things I wasn't supposed to want. She told me all the bad things I knew, deep down, were in me. She knew exactly what I wanted and told me she could give it, if she wanted to. I loved it and hated it. My mind surrendered but my body fought and we danced back and forth in hot battle. There was biting, hair pulling, slapping and scratching involved. We covered pretty much every surface of the room. My injured cheek burned but so did the rest of me so it didn't matter. Despite the pain there was some healing going on inside of me.

Later that night I woke with a start. A panic hit me. What if they knew where we were? What if they were coming for us? Debra lay beside me. Motionless save for the rhythmic rise and fall of her chest. Relaxed as if she were asleep, eyes closed but no movement underneath the lids - not dreaming.

I sensed she wasn't asleep. It might have still been part of the dream that I slipped immediately back into but I sensed that she was waiting. More than that. I sensed she *wanted* them to come.

Chapter 24

When I woke I rolled towards Debra and put my arm round her. We kissed for a while but she wasn't having any of the other. Once the cloud of sleep had lifted from me and we were sat up she said to me, "They were the guys that attacked Kel weren't they?"

"Two of them certainly fitted the description that Daz gave me of the guys who left the club after him."

"Are you going to go to the police?"

"Yeah. I should have called them last night but I wasn't up to much."

"You didn't do too bad."

I was glad the humour was still there because her intensity could be quite scary. My focus was on finding Francesca right now but it seemed to be tying in with everything that had been happening up North. I was worried that Debra's only focus was finding and destroying her brother's would-be killers.

"But first I've got to hire a new car."

"You could use mine if you want."

I shook my head. Humour was one thing but that suggestion was beyond a joke.

As I showered, the dressing on my cheek got soaked and came off. I just put a regular elastoplast on it and hoped for the best. I enquired at the reception desk about car hire and they gave me directions. Debra dropped me off at the place and I asked her to go and scope a section of road that I'd seen yesterday from Hod Hill. Thinking back, there was something odd about the view of it I'd seen from the hill. Rather than run an obvious route across the bottom of the valley it seemed to snake off in a different direction. If it hadn't have done, it would have been a more obvious candidate for a route into D'ancona's domain. There had to be another way.

There was no way he'd have taken his flash car along that muddy track. Even if he didn't get stuck, the car would end up looking like a bugger by the time he got to wherever the hell he went.

The hire place had a reasonable range. I thought about a four-wheel drive but I'd had enough of mud tracks for the time being. I thought about maybe an armoured vehicle or a Chieftain tank. Great for storming the palace gates but a bit obvious for surveillance work. Still, all the driving was getting to me so I wanted something with a bit of muscle and comfort if at all possible.

"What's the fastest thing you've got?" I asked.

The proprietor motioned me over to the window of the office and pointed it out. It was metallic blue and its shape reminded me of a carving knife.

"That's our Vauxhall Calibra. 2 litre 16 valve engine with 200 bhp. It has a six-speed gearbox and four-wheel drive. Road legal Rally Car. Only better-looking."

"Can it keep up with a DB7?"

"Not in a million years, sir."

"Can it outrun a Nissan Micra?"

He just laughed.

"I'll take it."

"It is our most expensive rental, sir."

"Money no object," I said, cracking a smile that reminded me not to get too amused at myself until my cheek had healed some.

Maybe the elastoplast made me look cheap. If only he knew. Detective to the millionaire set, me. As if to ram the point home, he reminded me that I was to use super-unleaded for optimum performance and to return it with the tank full. Then I headed back to Blandford nick, took a deep breath, went in, and reported yesterday's events. They were not happy with me.

They wanted to know why I hadn't been in straight away last night, what I'd been doing on a private road in the first place - that kind of thing. They seemed far less interested in descriptions of my attackers and their vehicle. At least CID weren't knocking it back down to uniform this time.

I was sitting upstairs with a DI Sanson and a DS Blenkarn. The two were both perhaps in their mid fifties, world-weary, and would have made quite an entertaining double act on any other day. We weren't in an interview room, just an open plan office. They'd taken what I could remember of the Challenger's registration number - which was a fair bit under the circumstances, but then you tend to get good at things like that in my business. Blenkarn said he'd check it out and went off and mumbled something down the phone line. Ordering pizza for all I know. Then they grudgingly went through the mug shots, if only to humour me.

The two from Zeds weren't there but Big Ears was.

"Connor Kenzie," said Sanson. He seemed to say it to himself.

I didn't think I'd get even a name out of them but Sanson continued as if I wasn't even there. "Only ever got him for receiving, driving without insurance and unlawful assembly that one time. He's a pit fighter, though. King of the Gypsies and all that bollocks. Undefeated. The man's a killer."

"Yeah? Well I kicked him in the head."

Sanson looked me up and down before replying. "Hard man eh? I'm pretty sure I could take you."

"So could I," said Blenkarn.

"Me too," said the lanky kid from downstairs who was hovering around the door for some reason.

"No you couldn't," we all turned and said in unison. He shrugged.

"I'd let him take me," said a female detective from across the room. I flashed her a winning smile but the boys just glowered at her and she cast her eyes back at the desk she was working on. Round the edge of the desk though I saw her giving them the finger.

Lanky chipped in then. "That info you wanted on a

Challenger? Reported stolen last evening but the owner reckons it could have been taken any time. He says he didn't use his car all day and only noticed it was missing later on."

"And you came all the way upstairs to tell me that?"

"It was either that or go to a call box. No one ever answers the internal phone up here." And with that he left.

"What about the crime scene? Anyone going up to take a look?" I asked.

"It's not a crime scene until we decide that it is," said Blenkarn.

"*If* you had reported the incident somewhat earlier, Mr. O'Brien, then perhaps we would have rushed out to obtain physical evidence. As it stands, the rain will have taken care of everything." Sanson again.

"May have. But if it has then it would have done anyway regardless of how quickly I got here, and you know it."

"Let's get it over and done with then. You coming?"

"I wouldn't miss it for the world."

"And I suppose you'll be needing a lift?"

"Yes, I will," I lied.

So I directed them from the back seat of their knackered Montego to the place and guess what we found.

Nothing.

The wrecked car was gone. They were all raised eyebrows and corner-eyed glances. I wouldn't have been surprised if they started tapping their fingers against their heads in a "He's mental" gesture.

It was a while before I could even speak. What was noticeable though were the number of overlapping tyre tracks. Big ones. Like a tractor.

"I reckon it's been dragged away by a tractor, dumped elsewhere, and then the tractors came back and forth to wipe out any sign of my car having driven up here. Why else would there be so many tracks?"

"O'Brien. This is a farm track! Why on earth wouldn't a tractor drive up and down it?"

"Are you going to search for it?"

"All we have is your word. How do we know you are not just attempting to wilfully harass the landowner with an unwarranted police presence? Thereby wasting police time? I believe we also need to start thinking how you might come to possess detailed knowledge of a vehicle reported stolen last night."

"Oh, I'd come and report myself for that would I?"

"I think you just need to go home and forget about all this, because that's exactly what I'll be doing."

I wanted to rant at them but there really didn't seem any point.

"Well, at least you can't do me for trespassing on a private road any more."

We didn't say much on the way back in the car. They asked me to come back upstairs and then grilled me for full details of where I was staying, how they could get in touch with me if they required, places I'd frequented where I might have come into contact with Mitsubishi Challengers and big-eared boxers. They were just trying to make me feel small by then. I gave them the basic details. I didn't mention Debra or my trip to the car hire. I asked them whether they'd checked out the telephone number in Chelsea that Fran had given to the school. They told me it was a empty flat for rent which still had a phone line, that Francesca had probably just come up with a plausible sounding number. I asked them if they had checked out the letting agent, the previous tenant, the phone account holder. They just told me to leave then.

On the way out the female detective collared me and apologised on behalf of her colleagues. She said they were good blokes really but they'd both lost promotions whilst investigating matters that were a bit close to home for the questions I was asking. I told her that it didn't have to mean they lost their spirit too. She didn't have a reply to that but she did say, "It's my lunch break. Have you eaten yet?"

It was a good offer. Especially for the purpose of any info I might be able to charm out of her. But I had other plans.

"Sorry, babe. Some other time. I've an appointment right now - an appointment with Crime."

Chris O'Brien - Man of Mystery and Gritted Determination.

Then I went and blew the whole image by tripping on the way down the stairs.

So there I was, sat in the car. Hungry but not risking a move from my position. For one and a half hours I numbed me arse until the double act emerged from the Nick, got into their bucket of a Montego, and pulled away from their parking bay.

Then I followed them to see what I could see.

They didn't seem to notice me and we ended up outside a builders yard. Out of town but not completely in the sticks, there were several other industrial units such as a scrap yard and a tool hire firm. There was a dilapidated public house, a newsagents and an old building that looked like it had been turned into flats. There were enough cars about for me to cruise past, double back, and park up without looking suspicious.

I watched them enter the yard from where I was parked and then sneaked up on foot and had a nosy round the side of the gate.

Parked up beside a large portacabin was the very same Mitsubishi Challenger. Stake my life on it.

Just then my mobile trilled into action and I legged it back to the car so as not to be heard. It was Debra. "China, I think you might want to come take a look at this."

I was intrigued about the builders yard but that wasn't going to vanish into thin air. The Challenger was a different matter, but I had no idea how long I'd end up waiting to see if it went anywhere else. I'd come back to it. I agreed to meet Debra at a roadside café we'd seen the other day. Not long after she rang off, Sanson and Blenkarn came out and drove off. That was quick. No in-depth interrogation there then.

When I got to the meet I could have quite fancied a bacon sandwich but there was naff all that Debra could have so we both went hungry. I guessed that those two were probably back at the Nick by then. I rang the front desk. "DI Sanson, please. You might want to put me right through to his direct line; you know what he's like at answering calls from the desk."

And they did.

"Sanson."

"It's O'Brien. I just wanted to follow up on the Challenger. Worried that I'm still in the frame. Heard anything?"

"How did you get this number?"

"Talent."

"It just so happens that the owner has retrieved the vehicle himself. Found it parked a few streets away, keys still in the ignition. It happens."

"And you'd believe that on the strength of a phone call? How do you know it's not the thief just phoning up pretending to be the owner so you'll take it off the PNC? You people are…"

"O'Brien, we are not half-wits. We have of course visited the owner, checked that the vehicle was indeed *in situ*, and confirmed registered ownership."

"Oh. I'm sorry. My apologies. My mind is at ease." And I hung up.

So it was a visit to the owner. And if it turned out not to be I had caught him in a lie. All I needed to know, half-wit.

"Happy in your work?" enquired Debra.

I told her all about the morning I'd had.

"Poor you. Should I have come with you after all?"

"Yeah. You could have done the Jedi mind trick on them. *Yes Miss Prentice, it does appear very suspicious. Yes, we will investigate fully.*"

"Either that or accuse them of institutionalised racism."

"Let's continue to reserve that option."

We got on and drove out to the place she wanted me to look at. I'd probably been past it at least twice during the time I was down here. It was a lay-by/turning area on the hilly side of the road. It went all the way back to a rockface in the hill, like a mini quarry. Between the road and the rockface was a clump of trees and unless you made a point of driving or walking round the back of them you wouldn't see it.

There was a great big iron door filling a hole cut into the hillside. Big enough to drive at least a Bedford van through. It was the shape of the Arch window from *Playschool*. Thick and heavy. Didn't give and rattle when I pounded on it but boomed with an indication of the hollowness behind it.

Without saying a word we both started to scramble up the rockface on either side of the door. It was maybe thirty-five, forty feet to the top. I've scrambled over every inch of the Cow and Calf on Ilkley Moor and I'm pretty quick at free climbing. It's the only way I know how. Pause to think and I get stuck.

Debra was already there waiting when I reached the top.

We were now on a grassy plateau that stretched away for a good hundred yards before it dropped back to the level of the road we had climbed up from. The earth was soft and spongy with previous rain but with a rebound underfoot which spoke of the immobile rock beneath. Beyond the drop there was a single track road in pristine tarmac. The road headed all the way up to a big house partially obscured by trees. It was the house from yesterday.

I stared at the scene for a while, ran my hand through my hair, and spoke. "I don't believe it! He gets to his house by fucking tunnel!"

"Probably got a cave and a butler called Alfred," said Debra.

Chapter 25

It was around two in the afternoon by then and the winter sun was doing the best it could for a change. The urge was strong to just hang around up there for a bit, collecting my thoughts. Then I realised that our two figures would have been standing out in bold relief against the white sky to anyone watching from the house, so we climbed back down.

We both got polystyrene coffees from the small caravan that smelt of fried onions, white bread, bleach and cling film. Though the sun was still strong, it was just starting to spot with rain from God knows where, so we went and sat in the Calibra, the more comfortable of the two cars.

"So what do we do now?" asked Debra. I think she had been watching my cogs whirring.

"We exploit our new discovery for the purposes of gathering intelligence," I replied.

"Go on."

"We stake it out. Keep it under watchful eye. Determine who or what is going in and out. What times of day? Which direction do they go in when they leave and come from when they return? How does the door open? Inwards or outwards? Automatically? Manually? Whatever we can find out. We take pictures too."

"Are we looking for anything in particular?"

"We don't know until we see it. Enough coincidences have piled up to make this worth doing but we still don't know anything. I couldn't swear that it was an Aston Martin in that garage. If it is, it still might not be D'Ancona. If it is him then he still might have nothing to do with Fran's disappearance."

"But the guys who attacked you...?"

"Yeah. I think it all ties together. But I don't know how, why or what I'm supposed to do about it. I can't just walk in there and tell him to confess. Best case scenario with this stake out is that the pair of them come driving out of there, Fran holding the door open for him, we snap it, give the picture to the police and force them to do something. Worst case scenario - nothing at all happens."

"No. Worst case scenario - we get spotted doing the surveillance and they come kill us."

"Yeah. That had crossed my mind, but I was just trying to be upbeat. This might be the right juncture for you to call it quits and go home. You've been a great help, Debs, but I won't judge you if, at any time, you want out."

"No retreat. No surrender," she said, only half joking.

"Cool. There is another lead I want to follow up. The Challenger and the builders yard."

"What do you want to do?"

"That's it, I'm not sure. Stake it out a bit, but maybe follow anyone I see leaving, maybe break in after dark and have a look around. I won't know until it happens."

"Fluid. Adaptable. Reactive. Like water flowing around a rock," said Debra with a smile that made me want to take my clothes off.

"Whilst surveillance on the door is more like the rock itself. Solid. Static. All-seeing. Recording the passage of time as the world moves relentlessly around it," I replied.

What were we like, the pair of us?

"The Yin Yang Detective Agency," said Debra.

"That's us, babe."

I left her with the Minolta and advised her to put the car elsewhere. We wanted to start tailing D'ancona, but not necessarily immediately, and if the car wasn't visible initially then that gave us a better chance of not being spotted once we started. I advised her to keep her mobile on vibrate if it had it, or its quietest ring if not, and to be far enough away from the door to be able to have a conversation without being heard. Both our signals were strong here. The position where I'd been attacked was a good two miles south east and the place where Debra had picked me up from was over the other side of Hod hill.

I drove off and found a health food shop. I got Debra a big bag of 'sticks' made from chickpea flour and sesame oil; two buckwheat pasties - mushroom & hazelnut; four organic apples and a litre bottle of spring water. Then I went and got another camera. Nothing flash - just something I could snap with if I needed to. I figured that Debra's surveillance was more pertinent.

Then I drove back and parked by the roadside cafe once more. I got them to fill my thermos with their appalling coffee, got a dirty look when I asked them to make it stronger. Debra's car was still there but we were across and down the road from where the door was and not visible from there. I decided to have a look around and see if I could find her. The obvious place would have been the clump of trees directly facing the door. A good view, just enough cover but uncomfortable and a bit too close - you'd be almost on top of the mark with not much time to get out of there if they 'made' you. A better place was a rock outcrop fifty yards to the left of the door. Good view again, much more comfortable with plenty of room to shift around, more escape routes. I looked around for a bit more. Still couldn't find her. I texted her:

I giv up, wer r u?

A minute later I got the reply:

On ridge 20m NE of dor

At first I thought it was a ridiculous place: too exposed and virtually no view of the door itself. Then I climbed up to meet her and realised it was almost perfect.

She had chosen a dip in the ground that had formed where large rocks seemed to be pushing through the grassy surface and this hid her from view if anyone had been looking from the house; which I had thought might be a problem with the ridge at first.

You couldn't actually see the door from where she was but Debra explained that she could see anything coming from the house, had a good view of anything approaching on the main road from the north, and a reasonable view from the south. She said that she had timed herself and was able to crawl into position above the door in readiness for any approach.

She was grateful for the tucker and looked really cute sat eating a pasty, her pretty features just peeking out from the hood of the large dark green waterproof that was covering every bit of her as she sat crossed-legged. Jeez. I'd be doing my bit from the car. I said I'd take over from her tomorrow but she said she was fine.

It would be dark in less than two hours. Although that shouldn't necessarily put you off maintaining your position on surveillance. I told Debra she could knock off whenever she wanted. I made the offer again of coming back to the hotel but she shook her head. I started to worry that she was actually going to stay out there all night.

So I got. The Challenger was still at the yard when I got there. I suppose I was working on the basis that the heavies were more likely to be where their ride was rather than hanging about at the house without it. That was what made me feel okay about leaving Debra where she was.

The builders yard didn't seem to be doing any business. There was no company logo or sign proclaiming their wares; just various piles of breeze blocks, bricks and gravel lying around. Parked next to the Challenger was a blue Transit and round the back of the portacabin there appeared to be a large wagon. The front gate was pulled to but not locked and the light was on in the portacabin, so I presumed someone was still around.

I sat and waited. The streetlights hummed as they powered up from pink to pale orange and I was reminded that, at this time two weeks ago, Tim Marconi had turned up in my office with some simple job about checking out drug rumours at Club Zed.

Since that time, I'd seen my first dead body outside of

161

nursing; my best mate had almost been killed; a friend's daughter had gone missing; I'd almost been killed; I'd lost my beloved car and Tim was heading for the Booby Hatch. Oh, and I'd met the love of my life.

By half past five it was well and truly dark and I was wishing I'd bought something to eat myself. Even hippy food would have been something. Didn't even have my thermos now. The Lord must have smiled on me because, right then, four men emerged from the portacabin, the last one turning the light off as he went. The last one happened to be that fat trucker Smudge. Two of them were my attackers, the other guy was maybe fifty odd, skinny but mean looking behind his glasses; his skin appeared to be weathered and impregnated with a wealth of dirt. Couldn't see his teeth but I'm betting they were yellow. If he had any.

Connor Kenzie, the big-eared thug, was not with them.

They all got in the Challenger bar the older guy, who locked the gate after it trundled out and remained idling at the kerb until he, too, got in and it set off. I waited until they got to the top of the road and turned left before I powered off after them. I knew the lie of the land now and reckoned I could have them in sight before they reached any other turn-offs.

Do you know where they ended up? Safeways. That's what I meant about the Lord smiling on me. When they went in I was able to pop in the front bit where they sell cigs, drinks and sandwiches and grabbed myself a chicken tikka salad baguette. I walked along behind the checkout like I had a purpose and managed to clock them out of the corner of my eye. They were in the booze section and all seemed to be choosing their favourites, adding them to a trolley which contained a couple of 24 packs of some cheapo lager. Couple of bottles of mouthwash scotch in there too. Looked like they were set to party.

I tailed them back to the yard. Well, not all the way. When

it was obvious where they were heading I parked up just beyond the top of the road. There was a bit of waste ground you could nip over and get across to the yard. It was one of those areas filled with rubble that used to be something. It was bordered along one edge by the side of a building. In the darkness you could just make out features of a past existence: remnants of splintered wood that had once been floorboards; ghostly patterns left by wallpaper long gone now; the bricked up outline of a doorway looking nonsensical - halfway up a wall.

I pressed myself into the shadows of bricks and mortar. No rain now, only cold indifferent wind. I visualised that where I was standing may once have been a warm living room. I closed my eyes momentarily and a family of happy, friendly, non-violent-crime-committing, pre-war ghosts sat down to tea in front of me.

Back in the land of the living I could see through the gate of the yard that they were lugging the booze out of the car. I presumed it was into the cabin, though I couldn't see from this angle. They all left soon afterwards. The Challenger stayed inside the yard and I didn't hear anyone setting an alarm on it. The older guy locked the metal mesh gate and they headed off on foot. I was going to head off after them once they got to the top of the road but we didn't get that far. They all piled into a decrepit, poorly illuminated little boozer on the corner. Obviously off for a livener before the serious drinking commenced.

I sauntered across to the yard, pulling my gloves on. No obvious alarm systems or cameras. Rattled the gate, didn't hear a dog. A security light above the cabin went on but then they do that all the time, don't they? Up and over. Easy does it. Maybe these guys were immune to crime on their own manor.

Round the back was the Volvo truck I'd seen on Sunday, this time with trailer attached. The cabin was old but large. Wooden steps led up to the door, whose Yale lock yielded nicely to a combination of picklock and credit card. I kept my Maglite low and moved it very slowly around the room. A free standing gas heater was on, keeping the place warm. The drink was piled up on what looked like a card table, confirmed by the presence of a couple of well thumbed decks lying there too. Adorning the walls were selected pages of *Razzle*, not even a clip frame to their name, hanging loosely by drawing pin alone and rustling in the draught that was managing to penetrate from somewhere. Probably the only thing that did get to penetrate around here, I mused. There was one armchair, enough straight back chairs for a decent card game and a swivel chair at a desk along one wall. On the desk was a telephone, a biro and a notepad. Minimalist gangsters.

The notepad was blank but there was an impression of writing left there from whatever had been torn away previously, like someone very heavy-handed had been taking a phone message. Yeah, like someone with twenty-five stone of flab bearing down behind their sweaty pudgy hand as they wrote. I could make out the impression easy in the strong beam:

Fri

10pm

Bridport

I 1471'd the phone. I recognised the number. At first I just knew I knew it but then I knew where I knew it from.

It was that number in Chelsea.

Apart from the testimony of three schoolgirls, this was my first solid link between Francesca and D'ancona. Albeit via Smudge. Still nothing I could get the police to act on, though. They weren't going to run down here on my say-so, press 1471 and go "Oh? Yeah!".

I'm not proud of the next thing that happened.

Well, to be honest, I am slightly proud. I just acknowledge my stupidity and recklessness into the bargain.

It started off as an accident anyway.

The sleeve of my Schott jacket brushed past one of the

164

scotch bottles and it crashed to the floor. Torch light reflected up from the shards of broken glass in random dancing patterns as I examined the whisky spilling across and soaking into the cracks of the wooden floor. As a slim trail of the stuff worked its way towards the gas heater like a lava flow in miniature I thought to myself how daft they'd been to leave it burning unattended.

I don't remember making a decision about it. I just know that I pushed the armchair up against the heater and upended the second bottle all over the seat. I was humming 'Streams of Whiskey' by The Pogues. Then I rolled up a few sheets of notepad, stuck them into the grill of the heater until they caught, and dropped them onto the chair. The flames were arm-length from the word go, the fabric of the chair melting and beading, exposing the yellow foam which instantly darkened and began popping with tiny black bubbles.

I lingered for a couple more seconds, feeling the heat on my face.

By the time I'd made it onto the rubbled wasteland again I looked back. There was an orange glow coming from behind the wall of the builders yard and a crackling sound that seemed to resonate with something primal and barbaric in me. I was grinning.

Card game's off tonight, lads.

As the gas cannister blew I could hear its muffled blast, then the splintering and buckling of the wooden structure around it. Like the shockwave bang of a firework, high in the sky, followed immediately by the rippling of its burning entrails, fading as they fall to earth.

And like a child on Guy Fawkes night I laughed with excitement. I couldn't have stopped myself if I'd wanted to.

The front of the cabin came into view through the mesh gate. I could see it now because it was moving. It toppled in a mess of blazing planks right into the back of the Challenger. And stayed there, dripping blazing gobs of bitumen which spattered over and around it - like flour from a sieve. Immolated wood hissed and crumbled into embers behind it. I could see strong flames licking up, fluttering like flags in the wind, from under the rear wheel arches.

It was beautiful. I almost took a photograph.

People were beginning to spill out of the boozer now for a look see. I walked back through the shadows and drove unhurriedly away from the scene.

Once I'd got out onto the open road I gave it a little gas just from the pure thrill of it all. I hadn't managed to salvage any tapes from the Escort so I stuck the radio on. If I was still being smiled on then maybe it would have been an appropriate track by the Prodigy or Jimi, or even The Crazy World of Arthur Brown. But no.

Although he'd been with me earlier I guess the good Lord thought I'd gone just a little too far this time.

Chapter 26

I think I've already mentioned that I'm not really into speeding but then I'd never driven anything with a six speed gearbox. It's pretty addictive. That feeling of completion you normally get shifting up into fifth, like an aeroplane levelling out and cruising above cloud level until it's time to descend? Sixth takes you beyond. Into the thin air of the stratosphere where the sky darkens and you see the curve of the planet below.

Alternatively, it's like turning the amp up to eleven.

I did mean to pull over and give Debs a ring but being just a little wired I pressed on and arrived at the Talbot, the pub where I'd gone with Jennifer. From the car park I phoned Debs, "How's it going?"

"Seen him twice."

"That's good going, probably it for the night."

"How can you be sure? We don't know what his night time habits are."

"Puts on a cape and fights crime? Don't over do it, Debs. Let's meet up and trade tales of our daring exploits."

"The first time was coming in. The second time was going out. He's *still* out."

"And may remain so. Mopping up the messes made by his minions no doubt."

"Are you drunk?"

"Not yet, but the night is young."

I gave her directions and she said she'd see me soon. Whilst getting myself lined up with a pint of Tanglefoot I made enquiries of the landlord as to whether he had any rooms. He did and I booked a double just in case Debra changed her mind later on. Hope springs eternal. Then I phoned the Crown Hotel to let them know I wasn't checking out but I would not be returning that night - didn't tell them where I was though. They thanked me for letting them know.

I was just getting started on my second pint when Debra arrived. Even though she was dressed like a hiker she still got the looks when she came in. I ordered her a coffee and we went and sat through in the chintzy dining area, perusing the menus. We filled each other in.

She had seen the Aston Martin returning to the house at around four. The door had opened remotely and inward. So no one got out of the car but it did have to wait a while as the door trundled open. Debs was pretty sure that the driver matched D'ancona's description and that there was no one else in the car. He'd left again around seven. That would be not long after the time of the fire.

I told her all about what I'd been up to. She was wide eyed in disbelief but reassuringly nonjudgmental. She was also interested in the Chelsea number so I held forth, "What I think is that it's just an address D'ancona keeps to pass messages through. They probably just had an ansaphone hooked up on the weekend that Fran was away, on the off chance. The place probably isn't in his name, not that the police seem to be bothered anyway."

"What about the note?"

"I'm assuming it's some sort of pick-up or delivery. The builders yard seems to have the sole purpose of being a parking place for that big rig. If Smudge is in D'ancona's employ, then we might assume that he is some sort of courier - but big style."

"What now?"

"I suggest we spend tomorrow keeping tabs on D'ancona, tailing him if possible. We can continue that the next day if we're getting anywhere, but in the evening we should try to find out what Smudge is up to in Bridport."

"That note could be a total dead end..."

"Welcome to Detection."

So it was agreed. Debra wasn't into staying at the Talbot.

She said she'd take the now empty room at the Crown but I told her that the only reason I wasn't staying there was that I considered it risky, especially after my little bit of payback tonight. I don't think she was bothered about the danger. Again I felt that a part of her welcomed the possibility of confrontation. I offered to pay for another room elsewhere but she declined. Independent woman.

It felt odd that she didn't drink whilst I was knocking them back. She was relaxed, she could act silly if she felt like it, but she remained completely in control. In previous relationships of mine, that had tended to be my role. It was difficult getting used to. I think I liked it about her. It's just the fact that we weren't trying to hop into bed with each other at every available opportunity that I really resented.

Still, there was a job to do here. And, when I really reflected on it, she was helping me. With more than just the legwork. She held a mirror up to me. She helped me to be more proficient, confident, to feel like I actually knew what I was doing.

When I first got into this business it was a gamble. I'd never done police or security work, just read a hell of a lot of fiction and watched a lot of telly. But I'd survived. I'd made up for lack of confidence with wisecracks and silly little business cards and I'd muddled through.

But this was different to serving writs or spying on crooked employees. Right now I was in the middle of the most scary and confusing situation of my life. Almost every second of the day I wanted to turn and run from it all. I also knew that I wouldn't run. Amidst all this I had *found* myself. I'd never been a good employee or team player. I'd come to feel that you end up serving whichever system you were working in rather than the people that it was supposed to be there for. But now here I was living the kind of autonomous life I was supposed to. I had a growing feeling that I was becoming closer to who I truly was. Wasn't sure if I was going to like myself as much anymore, though. What was I becoming? Apart from drunk, that is.

Debra was gone and my glass was empty. Now that *is* a spiritual crisis.

The bar gradually emptied and I enjoyed a cognac with the landlord. He happened to be called Mark. I started to tell him that I'd known a Mark. Mark Fawcett. Then I stopped myself. I was mistaken. I'd never known him at all.

Chapter 27

We met the next morning at the same place we'd parked before. The mobile cafe caravan wasn't there yet but I'd already got some breakfast at the pub. Don't know what Debra had done. Probably foraged for berries.

We staked out the road in both directions with Debra to the south and me to the north. We'd only seen him on the north road so far, so we thought that's where we should place the faster car. I parked up at the first exit on the left of the road and angled the car outwards to watch. The advantage of not watching the door was that D'ancona would be less vigilant once he'd actually set off. The disadvantage was that if I broke my concentration then I might miss him, flitting past on the road.

I felt like I was concentrating but you never can be sure as the hours pass. You can end up just dreaming that you're concentrating. But perhaps that's enough, as long as something nudges you from your dream in good time – the way dreams seem to naturally tail off until something in the dream world cues you to waken. For me it was the sound of the engine that did it.

Most of the noises from the road had been the constant hum of motors cruising past, already at speed. Every now and then you'd hear someone dropping down a gear or two to overtake someone else or, with the dampening sound of anchors being dropped over the lowered gears, slowing down to take the turn-off I was parked down.

This noise was different. The throaty growl of speed building, from not too far away. Full and rich and not laboured at all. As soon as it registered I had my key turned in the ignition. The Calibra was no slouch but its engine sounded like a wee baby in comparison. Albeit a very healthy baby that had had all its jabs and was now on solid food. The sound grew and filled the air. It didn't seem that he was slowing for the exit.

Before my wheels had left the grass verge, the DB7 flicked past in front of me. My mind took a snapshot like when you glance at the sun and turn away blinking. Though there was a slight tint to his windows I saw the driver. I didn't see any-one else.

Though it was a blind corner, I managed to check out there was nothing coming by scooting down the right hand side of the road to see as much as I could before gliding out to the left and onto the main road in second gear.

Then I floored it.

The DB7 was well into the distance, topping the brow of the slight climb to the north. By the time I was over it he was out of sight. He had vanished completely on a long stretch of visible road. Did he have one of those hyper-space but-tons? But there was another left turn between me and the horizon which I only became aware of when I caught a glimpse of him snaking through some winding roadside hedgerows that bulged from the landscape like veins on a bodybuilder.

By the time I had gotten onto that road myself I had given up hope of keeping him in sight. After about a mile and half of that windy lane I came to a T-junction and had no idea which way he'd gone. No tell-tale burnt rubber as the road was still wet from a burst of rain earlier that morning, and he didn't appear to have clipped the grass verge, leaving signs in the mud.

I drove carefully in each direction for a while, looking out for pedestrians, equestrians, cyclists who might have seen the distinctive car, but the roads were deserted that wet cold December day. And anyway, who's to say that the whole of chuffing Dorset wasn't in on the conspiracy? Ready to misdi-rect me at any given opportunity.

I phoned Debra and we met nearby. It was midday by then but there was no talk of stopping for lunch. We set ourselves up around the next exits so that we covered the four possible directions D'ancona could have gone in. I took what I thought was the more likely direction, the one that didn't look as much like he was doubling back on himself. Then it was just a question of sitting and waiting on the off chance that he returned the same way home he had gone; people often do. It was boring, though Mark and Lard on Radio One helped pass some of the afternoon. The other high point was a call I got on my mobile. It was Detective Sergeant Blenkarn.

"O'Brien. May I enquire as to your whereabouts last evening?"

"You certainly may. After taking an invigorating countryside walk I went shopping in Safeways. Later I repaired to a public house called the Talbot and drank some of your fine locally brewed ale."

"Hmm. That may put you in the vicinity of an arson attack on some property which took place last night."

"Really? Is there any reason to presume this involves me in any way?"

"It does seem to be related to some of the circumstances of your earlier complaint."

"That's very interesting. Perhaps you could tell me more."

"O'Brien, it's us who should be questioning you."

"Well, if that's what you wish to do..."

"The owner of the property, however, does not wish us to proceed with a criminal investigation. He assures us that the fire was caused accidentally by his staff."

"The owner being?"

"None of your business."

"Which begs the questions of why you rang me in the first place."

"Don't think we can't charge you with all sorts of things if we really want to."

And we kind of left it at that. I suppose that must mean

that they really didn't want to. I could live with that. Back to surveillance.

At around a quarter past four he came past me. Once more, I had heard him approaching before seeing him. He was coming out of a turning on my right, behind where I was parked. Again, if there was anyone else in the car then they were keeping well down. I didn't bother trying to follow him this time but I phoned Debra and suggested that she head back up her way to see if he went past her. If he didn't then it was just further confirmation that he was heading back the way he came. It appeared that he was.

Me and Debs met up again and this time went for a curry. I'm always reluctant to go for one out in the sticks. Tend to be overpriced and under-spiced. Coming from Bradford you can get pretty choosy. Anyway, it wasn't actually too bad. At least veganism didn't seem to pose the same challenges it did to an English menu. In this country, vegetables and pulses still tend to be treated as some poor relation that one speaks of only in hushed embarrassed tones.

We discussed what we thought might be going on. We were pretty keen on the idea that Fran was with D'ancona. Well, otherwise what were we doing? We also concurred that Fran had probably gone willingly, having established a relationship with D'ancona. Whether she now remained willing was another matter. There had still been no ransom demand but sometimes, speaking to Trevini and having nothing to tell him, I got the feeling that it would be easier on all of us if there had been.

I presumed that there was some manipulation of Fran going on. Knowing her, I couldn't see her being impressed with someone as dodgy as D'ancona. Therefore I guessed that he was hiding that side of himself from her. The fact that his shady henchmen had been hanging out at his pad made me think that she might not be staying there. He most likely had other properties where she could be staying. That's probably where he went to during the day.

Yeah. But Fran was either in on it to some extent or under some kind of duress by now, or she would have contacted someone. He seemed to be spending the best part of his day away from the house. Maybe on evenings too. Probably spending all that time with her to keep her sweet.

Well, it was a theory.

So. The next day we tailed him in the same fashion, this time from his last known vanishing point. Made a little more progress before losing him again but when we got together that afternoon and looked at the maps it appeared that he was driving into an area that seemed only to consist of private roads to farmhouses and such like. We might well be back to the same method we employed to find his main residence.

We spent a bit of time dozing on the bed then, back in the Crown Hotel. In each other's arms - which was nice. I had kept the room booked but had slept elsewhere again the previous night. It was now Friday and we had a 10p.m. appointment in Bridport. Exactly where and exactly why, we did not know.

Debs went on ahead and staked out the main road into Bridport which, as you've probably guessed, is a coastal town. Earlier in the evening I went to check out the builders yard. I couldn't help smiling. Whatever had been left of the Challenger must have been towed or dragged. A precarious pile of charred remains was all that was left of the cabin from where I was watching. The Volvo rig was there, its trailer hooked up. The only other difference was that the blue transit from yesterday was nowhere to be seen.

I waited until around half past seven when Smudge turned up in a taxi. I watched as he squeezed his bulk out of the back. The cab did a three point turn in the road and was off whilst Smudge was still delving around in his cavernous trousers. He finally pulled out a key and unlocked the gate before pushing both sides fully open. The wall-mounted security light had survived the fire and illuminated his path for a few more seconds as his overladen frame flopped towards the truck. Great waves of flesh seemed to undulate beneath his clothing as he moved.

I tried to analyze what disgusted me so much about him. I think it was because I really like my food and am prone to put on weight a little too easily. I have to constantly battle against it. Smudge, however, was in no such battle. He was sleeping with the enemy. So maybe I was jealous.

Shoot me if I ever look like that though, will you?

His beloved truck did not list to one side as he climbed up into it. Probably why he chose it. Quite a conversation piece too. Its engine rumbled into life and you could almost hear the National Grid tutting disapproval as his array of lighting bathed the dark misty air of the yard in iridescence.

I swear I had to squint as the rig rolled forward and exited the yard. I was glad to finally get behind him. He hadn't pulled up to lock or even close the gate to the yard. What was there left to protect?

And so I followed. Tailing an HGV in any sort of car is about the easiest job in the world. As long as you can ignore the hassle that other drivers give you for dawdling. You can stay far enough behind the truck for them not to be party to it.

He headed north, which surprised me as I'd expected him to go for the coast. After a few miles I sort of realised where we were, although we'd taken a different route to the last time I'd been here. At the back of the truck, the far less ostentatious brake-lights lit red, gears downshifted and a powerful hiss came from the air brakes as it swung out slightly to the right and eased around the left hand turn at the green set of lights. Didn't indicate. Tosser.

It was the transport cafe where I'd first met him. I didn't pull in to the car park after him as I'd have been way too conspicuous. I drove on past slowly enough to watch Smudge exiting the cab. The lights of the diner were on. I pulled over at the first opportunity in what looked like a farm entrance, hoping I wasn't going to be blocking any incoming tractors at this time of the evening.

I hopped the fence and made my way across dark wet grass to the slick gravel of the massive car park. Weaving in and out of large trucks parked in line, I felt like a small nocturnal creature making its way between the headstones in a graveyard. A fog was building up that night.

On one side of me were livestock. You couldn't even tell what kind of animals they were through the thin slits in the trailer, but light caught their blank eyes. There was hardly any movement, whether through overcrowding or sheer petrification. Steam rose from their hesitant, shallow breath and their urine, mingling with the mist. Their silence was scary.

On the other side of me was an open-topped trailer like a large industrial bin, loosely covered with a tarpaulin. Sticking from every gap between the material and the thick metal were the bones of animal carcasses. Some smooth and almost polished, pale yellow rather than white. Others had strips and hunks of flesh or tendon clinging onto them. The colour of the meat was green-grey rather than red. Like the hands of the undead clawing up from the soil. The smell went through me and actually hurt my head; it made my tongue feel like it was tasting something sweet but my nostrils burned and I resisted swallowing the saliva that was starting to flow. Parking the dead and the soon-to-be-dead right next to each other. How thoughtful.

I've never understood those people who see the life of the long distance lorry driver as somewhat of a romance. Perhaps there's autonomy in it - but at what price? God knows what the other trailers and tankers held. Vietnamese boat people and nuclear waste probably.

When I got close enough to scope the window of the diner it wasn't a great deal of use. The glass was all steamy from warmth inside and I could just make out the blurred shapes of bodies, some moving in front and behind the counter, most sat at tables.

What I did see was a blue transit parked out front. It was the one that had been parked in the builders yard two nights ago. I knew because I'd clocked the reg. It seemed to have escaped any obvious fire damage. Shame.

I stood for a while and was just beginning to become aware of my feet going numb when some guys exited the joint. Smudge was one of them, so was the dirty old man from the night of the fire, and Kenzie was there too. Weasel and Sideshow Bob were not. There were another five of them who I didn't recognise. Quite a mob. Smudge and two more got in the cab of the Volvo. Dirty piloted the transit, two getting in the front with him and another two climbing into the back. Obviously the two of lowest rank.

I set off in a gentle run for the car. I thought that I might not have time to catch the transit, but that I should be able to stick with Smudge still. I hoped they were all heading to the same place. Once I got to the car and set off I phoned Debra and told her to be on the look-out for the transit too.

I soon picked up the truck and settled into a gentle cruise way behind, heading south, and then south west this time.

Chapter 28

The drive took a little longer than expected but I suppose that was to do with my restricted speed. It was getting even foggier towards the coast although the wind was picking up too, so it came in patches. Swirls of the stuff rolled and danced before my headlights, buffeted by the currents of air. Pete Tong on Radio One was keeping me company for a bit but it was just too tempting to put my foot down to match the high bpm sounds. I switched to Radio Three and was greeted by Debussy's *'Dialogue du Vent et la Mer'*. Quite appropriate given the weather and the location I was heading to, but the music had a foreboding quality I could have done without.

As I was approaching a roundabout a little way outside the town Debra phoned. "Seen the transit, O.B. I'm following it now."

"Good. Try and stick with it unless it seems to be going anywhere secluded where you can't park without being obvious. I'll stay on the truck."

"OK."

We wound through the town following signs for West Bay. The streets were pretty wide through Bridport but got narrower as we headed down to the coast. It wasn't really a suitable place for HGVs but then I already had doubts about Smudge's sense of civic responsibility.

It soon became apparent that he was planning to park up as close to the small harbour as possible so I carried on past him and phoned Debra.

"Where are you now babe?"

"Pub car park. Bridport Arms Hotel. The transit parked here and five guys got out and went inside."

"Oh, I think I just passed you. See you soon."

I scooted around and shortly arrived at the car park. Debs got out of her car and into mine. Just then we saw Smudge and the other two guys approaching on foot and entering the pub. It was ten past nine now.

I had too great a chance of being recognised if I went into the pub, so Debs did instead. About ten minutes later she came out with a bottle of Newcastle Brown for me, a ginger ale in a faux ceramic bottle for herself and a big bag of kettle chips.

"Learn anything?" I asked.

"Heard them talking about a shipment. One of the guys said something about having to be finished by 2 a.m. I couldn't hang around any longer, I was getting far too many looks."

"Were you the only black person in there?"

"The only woman."

"Naa, surely not on a Friday night?"

"Well, the only one without facial hair."

I had to laugh. "So much for being inconspicuous," I said.

The night air had cleared around us but the sky above us was thick and few stars were visible. We seemed to be below the fog now, if that makes sense.

I put Radio Three back on. The music was still heavy with European romanticism but I knew it was not Debussy.

"Berlioz. 'Dream of a Witches' Sabbath'," said Debra absent-mindedly, as if answering my question. What well-rounded individuals the two of us were.

"Jeez. Fridays must be Foreboding Music Night."

"There's always the Essential Selection," suggested Debra.

At ten minutes to ten they piled out of the pub and headed toward the small harbour, all eight of them. We followed on foot, keeping quite a way back but walking briskly and holding hands like a couple on their way to the next pub on a cold night. When they turned down onto the jetty we walked straight past and then carried on a little way up the hill back into Bridport. Smudge had managed to park his truck right at the bottom and neatly heading upwards. God knows where he had turned it. It was the only time I caught myself admiring him.

"Let's double back a little further up, get the cars and park them on the hill. We'll have a reasonable view of what they're doing and we'll be ready to follow from further up town once they leave the car park," I explained.

So we made our way back to the cars, using one of the side streets higher up. Once parked up, this is what we could see.

There was a small commercial cargo ship squeezed into the port. It wasn't a great deal bigger than Smudge's truck. Cardboard boxes, roughly the size of old style picnic hampers, were being winched up from the hull through a hole in the deck. The small team of men who we had pursued were unloading them off the winching platform and onto trolleys which they then wheeled into the back of the truck. There was writing on the boxes but I couldn't see what. My Bins would have been useless in the dark. Perhaps I'll get night vision goggles if I ever hit the big time.

Another man, who looked like a cross between a night watchman and a customs official, was standing next to Smudge and holding a clipboard. They just stood and watched the rest of them working.

It took maybe three-quarters of an hour for them to finish. It was the winching that was the slow part. When it was all over they all, bar the customs guy, set back off towards the pub. One for the road? We had both been sat in my car to watch.

"Right, you get back to your car and let's head back up into town. The truck's the main thing to tail but if the van heads off somewhere else then you try and stick with it."

"If I'm on the van, don't I get the faster car?"

"No."

So we both drove back up the hill, pulling in on the wide main road with its darkened shops fronts, pubs and more chapel houses than I thought strictly necessary. There was a bit of a Friday night drinking crowd milling around and taxis doing deft U-turns every now and then. About twenty minutes later the truck lit the street like an alien abduction was in progress and chugged past, with the Transit close in behind it. I let one taxi get between them and me before setting off and I watched Debra fall in behind me in the rear view.

We were driving back into the fog but it was not as bad as before. Some of the brighter stars shone through every now and then. The truck and van seemed to be heading back the same way until just outside Dorchester, where they both parked in a truck stop behind a privately run petrol station that was now closed for the night. I carried on to the next roundabout, came a little way back and got into a residential side road. Debra parked up behind me and got out of her car as I did. She'd killed her engine but various clicks and rattles were issuing from under her bonnet, sounding like the mechanical equivalent of chronic obstructive airways disease.

"Shit car," I said.

"At least it's mine."

True. I missed my car, my black Ford Escort N reg with alloy wheels and one previous owner that had been my proudest ever purchase. I'd be mourning it for sure if there wasn't enough going on already.

I decided not to banter and just made a 'follow me' sign. We went down an alley between two semi-detacheds onto an old access road that had gone to seed with brambles and might well have been impassable in the summer. Anyway, we braved a few scratches peeking over a seven foot fence of gray warped timbers that smelt of dust. It blackened our hands and tiny splinters cut into our palms as we hung there but thankfully we had a great view.

The Transit was being loaded with some of the boxes from the trailer of the Volvo. We could see now that they were television sets of some new upstart Japanese or Korean company neither of us had heard of. When they'd done, four of them crushed into the back and three got in the front. Smudge got back into his cab alone.

"The van's where the action is. Let's follow the van!" I hissed through my teeth.

We both trotted back to the cars and both got into mine.

Smudge sailed past us at the roundabout, apparently heading back to Blandford. The transit was going the other way, towards the A37 and Yeovil. The roads were pretty empty by now. At night, you stay further back and follow the lights rather than the vehicle. It's a bit more difficult.

"What was that about? Why didn't they just load the van at the port too?" asked Debs.

"That maybe would have looked suspicious to the official that was overseeing them."

"Not as suspicious as what we just saw."

"True. But then no one was supposed to be watching."

The van turned off left after about ten miles. I speeded right up as it did and took the same turning. We were now going through one of the numerous hamlets around these parts, past a few cottages, a schoolhouse, a small cemetery. The van then turned off to the right on what we realised was a farm track as we cruised past the end of it. We could still see the van's tail-lights across the fields - and they appeared to be slowing. What I could also see now was a large hangar or barn looming on the skyline to our right. Wisps of cloud were all that was left of the fog now and moonlight glinted off the structure, showing it to be corrugated metal.

Suddenly, another patch of light, tiny in the distance, picked out the side of the building. It was the headlights of the van pulling up to it.

I parked at the side of the road, tooled up with torch and camera, and we got out.

"Silent running," I said, and switched my mobile off. Debra did likewise.

We headed off across the edge of the field towards the

hangar, out of sight from where their van was parked. I used the torch briefly, angled right at the ground, just to check how the going was underfoot. It was rough soil, damp but not muddy. It would have been some sort of vegetable field in the summer. Tiny flecks of stone sparkled in the moonlight, outside the beam of the torch, like the earth had been glazed. There would be a frost by morning.

We made our way slowly up to the opposite end of the hangar from where the van was parked. From inside the large metal structure we could hear mumbled voices and the chug of a small generator. Another higher pitched noise too. Maybe some sort of power tool. I eased my way, toe following heel, along the side until I could peek round the edge. Then I eased my way back to where Debra was waiting and said, "Sideshow Bob's stood at the entrance with his shotgun."

She didn't freak out or anything. Instead she just pointed upwards. I looked up and saw that there was an opening in the curving roof, a sizable metal outcrop like the attic window of a chalet. Some artificial light was shining out.

"I can't get up there!" I whispered.

"No, but I can." She motioned for me to give her the camera.

"Are you crazy!"

"Hey, I'm the one who goes camping in December, remember?"

"I suppose you'd have to be crazy to do that," I reasoned.

"Or just trying to prove something." She shrugged.

And that was the moment when a few things fell into place in my head. A few things that had been bothering me. I didn't say anything about it. Didn't want to complicate things.

I handed her the Minolta and she put it round her neck, letting it hang down her back so it wouldn't slap against the wall she was climbing.

"If they hear us before you get up to the top then drop

down and be ready to run the way we came. If they hear anything once you're up there then I'll draw them away and you just sit tight. Otherwise, don't come down until they've gone. One of the guys said something about finishing by 2 a.m. yeah?"

It was now just coming up to twelve-thirty.

Debra nodded and clasped two of corrugated ridges of metal that stuck out along the side of the building at intervals of just more than shoulder length apart. She began easing her way up in short silent bursts, using her feet as both stabilisers and brakes.

No matter how strong my grip, I couldn't have done that. At my body weight I'd have screeched and clanged, landed in a noisy pile and ended up with a shotgun up me arse. Debra, however, clung like a limpet. Sliding effortlessly upwards as if a magnet was attracting her from the inside. Kind of made me wish I was a corrugated wall. Once she got to the top, she poured herself into the roof opening, pausing to stick her arm back out in a thumbs up sign.

Then all I could do was wait. I kept my ears open for sounds. I wondered if the click of the camera might give her away if she was getting the opportunity but the generator was masking pretty much everything. I could hear raucousness in the voices from inside, but could not make out any of the words.

When the humming of the generator tailed off and sputtered out, I could hear bodies and objects piling back into the van and I looked at my watch. It was just coming up to half-past one in the morning.

Once the engine of the van was sounding well in the distance, Debs emerged from the skylight then did a hang, slide and drop that was pure Lara Croft.

"Well?" I asked expectantly.

"Half of the roof is a hayloft. I could see everything from where I was. They unpacked the TVs, dismantled them and took out the tubes."

185

"And inside the tubes?" I thought I already had an idea.

"Plastic bags full of white powder. Just like you see in the movies."

"You get photos?"

"I used the whole roll. Hope you don't mind?" She smiled.

"You beauty! I hate having to use the last few exposures taking pictures of my cat anyway."

We walked back to the car. The ground was rock hard now but I had a spring in my step. Debra turned to me:

"I don't feel like camping tonight. Do you mind if I come back with you?"

"Does the Pope shit in the woods?" I snorted.

"I've no idea. But after the past few days I've decided that shitting in the woods is overrated."

"Thanks for that mental image, Debs."

"Don't mention it. When we get back to the hotel I've got plenty more I can disgust you with."

My step just got springier.

And then I noticed that the ground wasn't the only thing that was rock hard.

Chapter 29

Saturday morning. I awoke smiling. When I looked over at Debra beside me the smile just got wider. I kissed her forehead and she opened her eyes.

"Let's run," she said.

No, it wasn't a euphemism. We togged up and took the same route through Bryanston's grounds that I had done on Monday. The sun had barely risen. There was still some ache in my upper left thigh from my kung fu kick but I didn't let it bother me. We matched each other stride for stride and the air was crisp and clean for a change. A frost formed a crust over the mud which crunched beneath us.

"You didn't go straight from school to Uni then?" I asked. I'd been thinking about what had made her the enigmatic character she was.

"SOAS is my second attempt. I started off doing English Lit. at Reading."

We kept our pace as we talked and neither of us were breathing heavily yet.

"What happened?"

"I was also doing a commission at Sandhurst."

"You were an army officer?!" I was incredulous.

"On my way to being. But it wasn't for me."

"I don't think I could do it either. I don't respond well to orders."

"As an officer you're supposed to give them. But I'm not a leader or a follower. I'm just me."

"So you gave it up."

"Hmm. Breaking the drill instructor's arm kind of forced the issue."

"I can see how it would."

"I don't respond well to bullying," she added.

We completed the run in silence. I managed not to lag

behind but, by the end, I was breathing a hell of a lot heavier than she was.

The shower we took together afterwards didn't help me breathe any less heavy either.

I had a real urge to get that film developed but there was no way I was going to hand it over to Boots or such like. The hotel obligingly put it in their safe for me and I loaded up a fresh one.

We studied the maps once again, this time downstairs on a convenient table as the last of the breakfast crowd trickled through. We were getting pretty familiar with the topography of the area by now, but, who was it who said "The map is not the territory?" Debra would probably know. Anyway, Bruce Lee put it just as well in *Enter the Dragon*: "It is like a finger pointing away towards the Moon." Meaning that the moon's the important bit, not the finger.

Our territory seemed to be down to about six square miles of what my old geography teacher might have described as 'delta', surrounded by rolling hills. We were going to have to cover it on foot. We divided the area up into six boxes and took three each in two L shapes that we would cover separately.

First we tried tailing D'ancona again, losing him where we'd lost him before but at least confirming that he was somewhere in that area. After that, we could only use the cars a tiny bit. If we drove blindly up too many tracks then we might just come face to face with him and the cat would be out of the bag.

By two in the afternoon I had been chased by a dog, stepped in two cowpats, but had been cheered by the sight of a fallow deer. This was a good couple of months before all that Foot and Mouth stuff kicked off, so luckily there were no Ministry of Agriculture officials hanging around ready to take me out with a sniper rifle. The trudging paid off though because, following the course of a slightly inclined private road by picking through the woods beside it, I could begin to see the dark shape of a house and what certainly looked like a sporty car in the shadow of it.

I had to stay far back and low because, being winter, the cover was sparse. No way I was going on my knees if I could help it though. My old combat trousers could have handled it. They used to have rubber pads sewn in at the knees. They've long since fallen apart at the seams though and I've never found another pair like them.

The ground was not particularly muddy but it was soft and the sense of wetness was enduring. I imagined that even in the heat of summer a dampness remained as foundation for the surrounding woodland. The kind of place that would be thick with mozzies. None of the trees were too tall so I imagined the roots weren't that deep either. Maybe a layer of rock beneath was waterlogging the land.

So there I was, crouching and sometimes kind of waddling, the sound of fast flowing water becoming louder, until I found a thick enough tree trunk to ease myself up against and watch the house from.

D'ancona's car was parked right outside the front door of a well-kept sturdy stone cottage. The door was squeezed into the left hand side of the building and the front window looked way too big for some reason. Every now and again a weak plume of smoke rose from a rectangular brick chimney. I guessed the building was a renovated water mill. A fence to the right side of the cottage bordered a babbling stream that took the slight downhill course of the private road away from it.

I wanted to get round the back of the house if I could, but the left side was too exposed. The route to the right still meant a dash across the road, going over a fence, across a river whose depth and width I could only guess at and then maybe back over it again to get round the back. So sod that.

I was running the idea through my head of just walking up to the front door and boldly announcing myself. Reckless, I know, but I was telling myself that I had every right to do just that. He was in the wrong, I was in the right, and Fran was too young to know the difference. Then I reminded myself that I still didn't know if he was visiting Fran. I could be walking into a well ordnanced crack house. Albeit a delightfully quaint one.

I resolved to stay where I was until he left before sneaking up on the place. I took a couple of pictures of his car in front of the house. Getting stuck right into the new roll. I tried to phone Debra but, as ever when you really need it, I couldn't get any reception. I tried a text message because they'll sometimes still work.

Greg here. Top left. old water mill? stream on map.

Text messaging: the modern equivalent of the carrier pigeon. I pressed send. Had an agonizingly long wait before hearing the most annoying electronic beep my ears had become accustomed to over the last year and seeing the irritating little 'stop' sign.

Message failure: the modern equivalent of the peregrine falcon.

I saved it to the outbox and kept trying to send every so often. I could have passed some more time playing Snake II or Racket but tried meditating instead. Tried to imagine that the tree I was leaning against was enveloping me in its aura and infusing me with its years of patient endurance.

But it was maybe only another hour before D'ancona emerged from the front door. He paused and turned and was followed by a second figure.

It was Fran.

My heart started to thump as if I had no chest muscle, only drum-tight skin. My mouth was instantly dry and perspiration emerged from my palms. It was the pure excitement that has no physiological difference from anxiety. I raised the camera and took about eight shots which captured them both together. Evidence at last.

Fran's long dark hair had been changed to a stylish fringeless bob. She was in jeans and T-shirt and minimal make-up.

She certainly looked as youthful as the last time I had seen her but was somehow holding herself in a more erect and confident way, like she had grown and changed. She looked serene and composed. They kissed for a long moment before he got into the car. It was all I could do not to throw a rock.

I typed another text message to send to Trevini:

Seen fran. she safe. wait dont ring.

I knew that he'd be craving for more but I didn't want to be getting into any in-depth conversations right now. I just wanted to get this sorted. This time the message sent. I forwarded it to Tim as well. I tried sending Debs again and this time it did but there was no delivery report like there had been with the other two. At least I could blame that on her phone rather than mine.

With the sound of the DB7 vanishing into the distance I hung the Minolta from a nearby branch. There's something vaguely seedy about having a camera slung round your neck and, if I was going to confront Fran, then I needed to give every inch the impression that I held the moral high ground here.

So I strode right up to that front door and knocked, like a friendly neighbour rather than a bailiff, and waited.

I heard some hesitant shuffling from inside, then footsteps coming to the door. She cracked the door cautiously and peered out but I was at an angle where she couldn't quite see me – not hiding, still a presence. The door opened a little more and I was ready with my Timberland boot but it wasn't necessary, she pulled it wide when she realized it was me.

"Chris!"

"Fran."

She stood and stared for maybe half a minute. I said nothing. Let her take the initiative, feel an element of control. Don't steam roller her unless absolutely necessary. Be Mr. Nice Guy. She might be more likely to open up about what the fuck was going on.

"I suppose you better come in," she finally said.

"I suppose I better had."

Chapter 30

The place was well kept and smelt of pot pourri. I think Fran must have concentrated on playing 'house' during what was looking like a self-imposed exile. The modern hardwood floor of the hall extended round into a very spacious living room as I was led by Fran through a wide doorway with recessed panels and heavy wrought iron handles. A fire smouldered rather than blazed in the hearth. Given the warmth of the place there must have been central heating too.

All the furniture seemed to be concentrated at the far end of the room, as if making way for something else, like a large dining table perhaps, but there was only empty space. It felt a bit like when a pub makes a sad attempt at having a dance floor.

I took up a position on the sofa. Fran sat opposite and just to the right side of me in a large armchair. Then she spoke. "I can't believe this! What are you doing here?" she asked.

"I've been looking for you, Fran. Everyone's been worried sick."

"Really? I don't think so. Who's everyone?"

"What are you talking about? Everyone who cares about you."

"Greg's the only one who cares about me."

Oh, please! Okay. Slow down O'Brien. Humour her.

"Right. Tell me all about Greg and how he cares about you then."

She sighed and for a moment there was a faraway look in her eyes. Then she sat up straight, put her hands in her lap, and fixed me with a look that was as if she was about to explain the facts of life to me.

"Greg and I love each other. We're going to get married. Dad's hardly likely to be pleased."

She was still maybe two and a half months from her sixteenth birthday.

"You haven't even contacted him. Does he deserve to be treated that way? How can you say he doesn't care about you!"

I couldn't believe what I was hearing from her.

"Packing me away to a boarding school. Is that caring for me? He never visits."

"You told me you love that school. And why would he come down and visit? You've never wanted him too. You visit back home whenever you want. What's all this about?"

"It's about no one really knowing the real me. Greg's the only one who understands."

"So you plan to elope? Get married when you come of age? Stay away from your father so he can't put a stop to it? What do you think this is doing to him?"

"It seems harsh, I know. But it is for the best. Nothing can get in the way of Greg and I being together."

I leaned forward and stared hard into her eyes.

"Fran. Don't talk wet. You're too young for all this 'true love' bullshit. Greg is using you. It's against the law what he's doing."

I realised that I'd lost her as soon as I said it. I'd undermined her and there was no way I could appeal to a sense of right or wrong. But I was getting pissed off.

She leaned forward too and there was fire in her eyes.

"I thought you were okay but you're as bad as everyone else. You speak to me as if I'm a child. Well, I'm not! I'm a grown woman."

She then sat straight in her chair and pulled her shoulders back as if to emphasise the point. Her breasts had indeed enlarged by about a cup-size since the last time I had seen her. Not that it was any business of mine.

"Put those things away. You'll have someone's eye out," I remarked.

It was hard for her to maintain her dignified manner at

that. She blushed a little and the corner of her mouth twitched like she wanted to giggle. Grown woman indeed.

I took the opportunity to change tack.

"Has Greg ever been up to Bradford?"

That surprised her.

"Yes. Yes he has. He went up on business a couple of weeks ago. He met you actually, but I don't think you'll have known at the time."

"Oh?"

"He went to Zeds one night. He phoned me and said he'd been speaking to one of the door staff. He described you."

"So you told him my name?"

"Yes. When he described you to me I said 'that sounds like Chris O'Brien'."

That's how he had known to ask for me on the phone that night then.

"Do you know what kind of 'business' Greg does?"

"All sort of things. He invests. He owns some racehorses, lots of property."

"Do you want to know what business he was doing in Bradford?"

"It doesn't matter to me."

"Well it should. Someone has been trying to systematically destroy your dad's livelihood. That someone is your boyfriend Greg."

"That's not true."

"He also deals drugs on a large scale. Fran, he's even involved in dog-fighting, for chrissakes!"

She loved dogs.

"Why are you saying this? Why are you being like this?" She stood up. She was trembling.

"Why doesn't he let you stay at the big house, Fran?"

A momentary look of doubt flashed across her face before she replied.

"This is where I want to be. You don't know us. You don't know me anymore!" She was flapping her arms now.

I stood up then. Like John Major, I didn't want to understand. I had come over all Zero Tolerance.

"Get your coat. You're coming with me." I nearly added 'young lady.

"You can't force me."

"Yes I can."

"No. You can't."

But the reply hadn't come from her. Standing in the double doorway of the room was Greg D'ancona.

Chapter 31

She ran into his arms. I stepped away from the sofa and into the centre of the room. She started to try and speak to him, to tell him all the awful things I'd been saying, but he shushed her lips with his finger. Told her he would make everything okay. Told her to go upstairs and wait until he came up to get her. She did as she was told. He was very slick and very convincing. Maybe he was just going to tell me to leave. Maybe I'd do as I was told.

He stepped towards me and there we were, with just over two arms lengths between us. We weren't going to shake hands.

"Very clever, O'Brien. Very perceptive."

"How much of that did you hear?"

"I've been listening in the hall long enough to get the gist. She's really quite fond of you isn't she? But you'll have gathered by now that her loyalties lie firmly with me."

"She doesn't *know* you, D'ancona. If she did, she wouldn't have gone this far."

"And do you feel you know me?"

"It was you who said I was very perceptive. It took me a while, but now I know what you're up to."

"Which is?"

"You're planning to kill Trevini. Not only that; you want to make it look like suicide."

"Really! And how did you arrive at this startling conclusion?"

"When I realized you'd done the same thing with your own parents."

He just smiled at me then. A proud smile. Like I was a teacher handing him some homework marked A-plus.

"I'm listening, O'Brien."

"It goes a little something like this. A young, intelligent,

196

but obviously twisted boy sees his family fortune slipping away before his eyes. He thinks he can do better than his parents. If they hang around much longer it's going to be gone for good. He decides to get rid of them. The conditions are right for it to look like suicide, so that's how he makes it seem. Maybe even helps the conditions along a little. What were you like to your parents in the final weeks?"

"Oh, I was perfectly awful! I was hardly ever there, and when I was I'd only be nasty to them. I told them constantly that they'd ruined my life, that I hated them, that they were useless parents."

"So in their darkest hour you systematically chipped away at their self-esteem."

"It helped that they were so weak to start with."

He said it with a mixture of disgust and pleasure. One emotion for them and another for himself.

"It didn't jump out at me immediately. What got me thinking was why you'd be away on a camping trip in the middle of December. What kind of eejit does that?"

Sorry Debra.

"I consider it the cleverest part. I'd been sleeping out in my tent a lot that month. It wasn't pleasurable but it served a purpose. The locals were used to the sight of me camping out in various locations by the night of their death. It wasn't suspicious to anyone. Afterwards I told the police that I was only doing it because of my parent's 'violent mood swings', I felt uncomfortable being around them, I felt rejected."

"A fourteen-year-old boy, orphaned, a week from Christmas. I bet they didn't go too heavy with the questioning did they?"

He just smiled. I continued.

"And being out camping gave you the perfect excuse for not having to account for your movements. Sneak back into the house without being missed by anyone. Be back in your tent when their bodies are discovered. I'm just at a loss to know how you got them to overdose."

He was so obviously proud of himself that he was ready to share it.

"I didn't creep in unannounced. I came and told them that I was sorry, that I loved them really, that I was just confused. They lapped it up. They wept for joy. I cooked them a meal, a peace offering."

"Oh, I see. Poison mushroom omelette?"

"A farmhouse stew. Befitting of their heritage. It contained some seeds of the ackee fruit, which release cyanogenic glycosides when crushed. I ate the same stew, but merely knew to spit out the seeds."

"Was the fruit a present from your Malaysian friend?" I chipped in but he just continued.

"It made them weak and ill enough to force the barbiturates down them. Some whole, some in solution. I watched them die before I left in order to prevent them seeking help or leaving a note."

The whole thing was sickening. But I forced myself to continue, as if we were enjoying a pleasant chat.

"So that was one little boy who didn't make Santa's list that year. And the little boy grew up to be a rich and powerful man. Then, as always in these stories, boy meets girl. In this story, girl has rich father. Boy plans to kill father and take over his business empire. Boy sweeps girl off her feet, manipulates girl into hating father, boy creates conditions that will make eventual death look like suicide."

I didn't bother to tell him how much of the psychic assault Tim seemed to be soaking up on Trevini's behalf. I just continued. "It's not exactly a fortune compared to yours. But I suppose any legitimate businesses are handy when it comes to laundering money from your less legitimate activities."

"And the north is the new south. Lots of growth." He shrugged.

"Yeah. I hear drug use is skyrocketing." He didn't appear to disagree. "But I think really you just wanted to play the same game once more. Just to see if you could."

"For all the money I've made, for all the men I've beaten in combat, I never felt more powerful than when watching my parents die. The moment I claimed my destiny."

He seemed to be talking to himself now.

Then he turned his full gaze to me.

"Killing you should be the most fun I've had in a while though." He smiled.

Chapter 32

He didn't pull a gun on me. I don't know what else he was waiting for. Maybe a trap door to open up underneath me and drop me into a shark-infested pool.

"I hate to disappoint you, D'ancona, but I'm not some poisoned junkie who can't defen - "

And that's as far as I got before I found myself on the floor. I hadn't even seen him move and I didn't even remember falling. It was as if I'd lost half a second of time somewhere.

I couldn't even work out if I was in pain anywhere. My brain wouldn't function. The air felt like glue and my vision blurred as I managed to figure out that D'ancona was standing over me.

"You've got a hard head, O'Brien. I normally break boards with that kick."

I started to scrabble to my hands and knees then. Fear was working my muscles for me, and not particularly efficiently either. I stumbled half upright. That was about the time my brain started working again and I carried on stumbling towards the corner of the room.

If I backed myself into a corner then that would negate a large chunk of his arsenal of spinny, kicky stuff. He'd have to come straight at me with linear movements. I must have looked pathetic bolting like that.

He followed me slowly, wanting to drag the fight out, wanting to have some fun.

He came in with some snap kicks and straight punches, with maybe half the speed and force he actually had. Letting me block him. Seeing what I had. I only let him see basic karate blocks until he came forward with a thrust kick. Throwing myself right against one wall as I pivoted to the side and did a *Wing Chun* leg trap, hooking under his leg with the crook of my elbow. My other arm snapped out to chop him in the side of the head but he blocked it with his forearm. By that time though he had no way of stopping me kneeing him in the back of the trapped leg. That put him off balance enough for me to tip him backwards and it was his turn to hit the floor.

I was way too slow to capitalize on it. He spun back up onto his feet before I could get to him so I just backtracked into the corner again.

He wasn't going to be fooled by a change of styles this time. He started launching full speed fists, knees and elbows at me. My blocks and parries weren't stopping him from hitting me, they were just getting in the way enough to lessen the impact. He was too fast to trap and I was getting weak. That's when he just slapped my hands out of the way, grabbed at my sweatshirt, pulled me towards him, and then slammed me up against the wall a couple of times. More school bully than martial artist.

You could say he paid for it because that's when I head-butted him on the nose. The thing is though, he just laughed. Then he did it back to me. I was in danger of passing out. I felt like I weighed an ounce.

But that's when Debra crashed into the room. D'ancona threw me to one side and turned to face her.

"And who is this?"

"It's a girl with a stick, Greg."

I was lying on the floor and talking bollocks.

Debra had hold of a hockey stick and was wielding it like a *naginata*. That's a Japanese wooden staff which is shaped like a hockey stick but much, much longer. Wouldn't fit in the back of a Nissan Micra for instance.

D'ancona shuffled towards her and drew her in. Debs started swinging the stick deftly and trying to clip him but was cautious. He was making grabs for it and she didn't want to lose it.

Then with the same surprising speed that he had kicked

201

me in the head, he spun low and swept her feet. She went down but kept the stick and rolled away.

By that time I was on my feet and charged him so he couldn't follow up on her. I ran right onto his palm and was straight back on the floor.

I get knocked down, but I get up again. You ain't never gonna keep me down.

Me and Debs were now double-teaming him. He was fast enough to keep us both at bay but couldn't commit his attack to either one of us. He had his eye mainly on Debra's stick and she certainly wasn't making any wild movements which might give him the chance to wrest it away.

It turned into a bit of a workout, there in the middle of that room. It could have gone on all night, except I was now falling apart at the seams. I wasn't faint anymore but my limbs felt like lumps of lead.

All the time D'ancona was grinning a smug grin. He was starting to ignore me all together and that really pissed me off.

I caught Debra's eye for a brief moment then shouted:

"Head shot!"

I launched a rugby tackle at him.

He covered up like a Thai boxer, forearms vertical in front of his face, hands facing outwards ready to grab, his left knee came up to cover his lower body. It was the smartest thing he could have done and I was ready for it. If I hadn't been ready for it I'd just have glanced off his knee. As it was, a couple of my ribs snapped like lolly sticks and I all the air got knocked out of my lungs but I held on as he went down.

Debra swung the hockey stick at his face, avoiding me as I went low. He took it on his forearms, which must still have hurt like hell, and managed to rip it from her grasp as he went backwards.

I ended up on top of him on the floor. I'd like to say we were grappling but really he was just crushing me into him and rolling around the floor with me. My arms were pinned like wings at my side and he was pressing the hockey stick into my lower back. The rolling was to ensure that Debra couldn't risk putting the boot in without getting me. Our legs were just flailing and knocking against the floor and each other. My only weapon was my chin which I was digging into his sternum for all I was worth. His chin was digging into the top of my head which felt like it was going to burst. My spine felt like it was going to crumble into powder at any moment.

I wanted to yell: "Go for his eyes!" but I couldn't manage a sound.

Momma Prentice didn't raise no fools though. I could sense Debs struggling above us as we rolled and then D'ancona shrieked in pain as she pressed her thumbs into his sockets. It was the most welcome sound I'd ever heard.

I don't care how hard you are. You can't put muscle on your eyeballs.

And as his grip loosened I pushed up and away, my fists at his throat and my knees driving into the muscles of his thighs.

And then we started beating that man like there was no tomorrow.

He was strong and he made a comeback at one point, pushing his back against the wall, lashing out through blood-clouded, stinging vision.

He caught Debra a punch that broke her nose; I know because I heard it and her blood splashed onto me as I fought besides her. I've seen big hard men sit out a whole session after taking a sloppy sparring jab in the same spot. She didn't slow down at all. She stomped his ankle as he slid back down the wall and that's when all the fight left him. We put in a couple more digs each as he sat propped against the wall, unable to raise a limb. I swear you'd have done the same.

At that moment the big double doors of the room flew open once more and in stormed D'ancona's three heavies who'd jumped me on the track.

And the Devil take me if we didn't beat them all to hell too.

Chapter 33

The small guy ran straight for Debra. Either he was scared of the same treatment I'd given him before or he was an Equal Opportunities Henchman. Her leg shot out into a piston-like sidekick which he ran straight onto, spearing him in the solar plexus. In a fluid move from the sidekick, her foot raked down on top of his kneecap on its way back to the floor – forcing his knee joint in the direction it ain't supposed to go with an almighty snap. His screech of agony was cut short by a spinning back fist to the side of the head which dropped him. I learned later that Debs had broken a knuckle doing that, so it must have really rung his bell.

That left the other two going straight for me. Two on one is not good. Your best chance is to make one get in the other's way. I took control by running at Sideshow Bob with the big hair and pivoting to the right of him as he threw a right. I did a *tan sao* block with my right whilst simultaneously smashing my left fist into his oblique muscle. This kept him on the outside right of my centre line and momentarily put his whole body between me and Connor Kenzie.

Controlling that blocked arm now by turning the *tan sao* into a wrist grab, I pulled him forward and down into a left elbow strike to his temple, that left my left hand to grab his right biceps and pull his face into my right elbow, my right forearm rolling round the back of his head to force his throat down into my rising right knee, which then raked down his leg, pushing him to the floor.

If you've never seen *Wing Chun* in action, then that will sound like utter bollocks. If you have, then you'll recognize it as a basic modular sequence of simultaneous counters and strikes that is over and done with in less than two seconds.

That two seconds was all that Kenzie needed to get his bearings and plant his feet. If his silly-haired mate hadn't been dropping to the floor by then I think he'd have picked him up and thrown him out of the road anyway. As it was, his big fist came sailing into view and he caught me with a looping right which would have knocked me down if I hadn't been taking an immediate back step from the last exchange. He'd have followed up quicker than I'd have reacted too if he hadn't had to step over a body to get to me. He closed the gap and followed up with a left cross which I managed to dodge and I stuck in two very quick right jabs to his left eye over the top of it, then a left hook to his mouth which rocked his head back and split his lip.

After my first flurry of *Wing Chun* I had lapsed into straight down-home pugilism. I always do. No matter how hard I try to be Chinese, it's an Irish roots thing.

Debra was down on the floor. She had the guy that I'd just dropped in a head lock and was choking him out. He was trying to butt her with the back of his head without success. Maybe because of all his hair getting in the way.

Kenzie put in a good combination but I blocked the first two and slipped the third. My right cross smashed through his guard and clipped his chin, my left found his stomach. I'd kept my broken ribs protected with my elbow throughout.

I closed in and threw another couple of jabs. He was on the back pedal and dodged them but he was going off balance. I feinted with the left and then put in another right jab that just found its target mid-cheekbone. Part of me knew that I had the perfect opportunity to either knee kick or shoulder barge him at that point and put in some finishing moves but I hung back and let him take a couple of wild swings which I had no trouble dodging. Undefeated King of the Gypsies. Yeah? I was going to out-box this fucker.

I didn't get the chance because by then Debra was back on her feet and took him down at the back of the knees with the hockey stick, kidney-punched him with its handle as he buckled, then, using the stick as an aide this time, put him in a choke-hold until he went limp. You find something that works for you, you stick with it.

Smashed knee weasel fella was still conscious but bleating in agony with a look on his face that said shock had taken him to a far away place. The objective part of me assessed that his need for medical attention was greatest. He might go hypo-volemic and probably needed to be on a drip as soon as possible. I sensed internal bleeding too. The subjective part of me couldn't give a rat's ass.

D'ancona looked alert in comparison. He was sat against the wall, glaring through blackened and rapidly swelling eyes. He could have made a run for it but, on that broken ankle, it would have taken him a week to get to the main road.

The other two were unconscious but breathing steady. They would be back with us in two or three minutes but wouldn't feel up to much when they were.

Good. They could all just go fuck themselves.

Debra was on her knees. Gasping, almost sobbing for breath. Exhausted. The bust nose didn't help either.

"O'Brien... you fight... like a... complete... *wanker*... don't you?"

"I was making out..." I said defensively.

She jerked her head towards the now prone Kenzie. "He was drawing you in and lining you up. His next punch would have killed you."

I just nodded. Try never to disagree with a woman who favours choke-holds.

I phoned 999 and asked for police and ambulance, giving directions to where we were. I didn't use my mobile - let it go on Laughing Boy's phone bill.

Debra was patting the vanquished down for any concealed surprises. She used one hand, performing a wicked wrist-lock with the other - even on the guys who were struggling to regain consciousness. Her nose was dripping blood as she did so and, every now and then, she gave a painful cough. But she remained thoughtful, precise, focused. Made me look like an arsehole. I was more in love than ever.

There was a lock knife in Weasel's boot. The only weapon we could find.

At some point, and there's no way I could have said which, Fran had come downstairs. She had come just inside the doorway of the room and stood like a frightened animal, her mind not allowing her to understand the carnage in front of her. Unable to run to her loved one's side. Unable even to run away. I moved towards her but she flinched and stumbled, throwing herself against the wall. I decided not to force the issue.

D'ancona watched us, rallying his thoughts. Finally he spoke.

"There's nothing to suggest to the police anything other than what I'm going to tell them: that you broke in here and assaulted us all..."

I shook my head.

"Bully for us. What's Francesca doing here? How do you explain that?"

"I let her stay here. Her life at school and at home had become a misery and she had no one else to turn to but the kind stranger she met once. She only turned up after the police had questioned me. Reckless of me but hardly criminal. How many different stories do you think we've already rehearsed to cover the eventualities, O'Brien? Isn't that right my love? Be strong for me."

I nearly kicked his face off at that. Fran said nothing. Pushing herself back against the wall like she wanted the molecules of her body to merge with it, become a ghost and fade away from the reality in front of her.

"What about your boys here? And everything they've been up to."

The two were starting to revive, but now the weasel guy had lost it. Poor love.

"If the police find any forensic evidence then good luck to them. I hold my hands up."

"You taught them well..."

He forced a smile through swelling lips. By God he was a smug git.

"He could be right, China. Perhaps we should kill him. Get what justice we can before the police arrive," said Debra.

Jesus. Was she just trying to scare him or did she really mean it? If Fran was going to stand by her man then maybe Debra was forcing psychological crunch time upon her. Throw herself across him or fly screaming and scratching at the female rival. Fran remained rooted. Good call.

Time for me to wrap this up. I put on the smuggest face this side of Jeremy Paxman and, with not a little air of ceremony, produced the smallest, coolest recording device you're ever likely to see from a tool pocket halfway down the left leg of my combats. It had survived the tussle. Its tiny green light was on.

"D'ancona. Just call me Inspector Fucking Gadget. Alright?"

If you could have seen his face. Priceless.

"I thought I might get a confession out of Fran but hey, these criminal masterminds just love the sound of their own voices."

I had out-psyched him. You might think it's contrived when the villain always seems to confess their wrongdoing. But it happens. There's a psychological need for disclosure. Call it revealing the *gestalt*, discharging guilt or just letting people know how fucking clever you've been. If someone knows they're going down with absolutely no doubt then they'll confess everything. Hell, they even do it when they're not guilty of anything. The power of suggestion. But he presumed in his arrogance that he'd be killing me so why not allow me to recognise his brilliance in my moment of transformation to the Divine?

It was still running.

"Anything you want to say to the jury?"

He looked like he was going to pass out. I glanced round at the beautiful Debra who shrugged and replied, "Hell, people. The bit about killing him? I's jus messin' wit ya."

I couldn't resist it.

"D'Ancona. You would have gotten away with it too, if it wasn't for us meddling kids," I added.

Faint at first, the oncoming sirens got steadily louder and pierced the silence that had befallen us all. Just before the first paramedic and police officer stepped through the door side by side, Fran came away from the wall, over to me, and held me like she was scared the wind would carry her away.

Chapter 34

After a brief explanation of the proceedings to the senior officer - a DCI who was accompanying DI Sanson and who looked like he'd been pulled away from a game of golf - they were keen to bundle us off to hospital. I insisted on retrieving my camera from the woods so a uniformed officer came with me. I couldn't see it anywhere but he eventually found it for me. For some reason I'd felt myself getting upset out of all proportion at not being able to find it. I knew it was irrational. But when the officer spotted it I threw my arms around him and started laughing for joy.

I giggled in the back of the ambulance almost all the way to the hospital until the post-fight chemicals that filled my bloodstream began to subside.

Our enemies were going straight onto the admissions ward under police guard. Me and Debs sat in an A & E cubicle with a female officer stood not too far away. The same officer had had to prize Fran out of my arms back at the house. She was nowhere to be seen now. She'd be at the nick in the company of an Emergency Duty Team social worker until such time as one of the family could be with her.

I noticed the laminated sign on one of the walls about switching your mobile phone off so dutifully I did so. But then I noticed something strange. My text to Debra still hadn't been delivered. She had never got my message about being at the house.

I turned to her, but just then a young George Clooney lookalike, his stethoscope at a raffish angle, came and swept her away.

Soon it was my turn too. I was poked and prodded and tutted at. I was asked if I was passing any blood but I said I hadn't had time to check. A quick trip to X-ray and then I was given a prescription for both Co-codamol and

Diclofenac to pick up from pharmacy. I would have liked them to tape my ribs but they don't really do that these days. I went to collect my meds. Twelve quid. I wasn't thinking straight so I just paid up. Could have gone to a supermarket and got the only slightly less potent equivalents for one pound fifty.

Debra was back in the cubicle when I returned. She had a small pot on her right wrist. The bridge of her nose had been glued and it looked about twice its normal size.

"Don't say a word," she mumbled. "The Doctor's already told me I look like Shaznay Lewis."

"Oh, flirting was he?"

"I guess he was, a little."

"Point him out to me and I'll go kill him."

"O'Brien. Right now you couldn't even kill time."

She had a point.

We sat next to each other in silence for a while waiting for instructions as to whether we were wanted for more treatment or whether it was time to go for questioning. I noticed we were holding hands but it must have just happened without me having to think about it - our hands were just there.

"Debra?"

"Yeah?"

"How did you find me?" It had been bugging me.

"I used my third eye."

"What? Is that like - my Spider Sense is tingling?"

"Sort of. Heightened awareness is common when a loved one's in mortal danger."

Loved one. I liked that.

"Debra?"

"What?"

"You're just as much of a wanker as I am, aren't you?"

"Could be!" she said. And she said it like Hong Kong Phooey.

But I never asked again and she never did tell. I've come to learn that, with Debra Prentice, you never really know.

Chapter 35

Both Tim and Trevini were down there and waiting for us by the time the police had finished with us. Or finished with us 'for the time being' as they put it. It was about 10 p.m. by then. As we walked out of the station, they headed towards a black Mercedes people carrier that appeared to have been rented for the occasion.

"There is someone with us to see you," said Trevini.

It was Kelp. He was sat in the back of the large car with his potted leg on a seat and his crutches leaning against the window. Even in the darkness he had shades on. He grinned wide and it didn't make him wince anymore.

Debs and I took it in turns to hug him, all cognisant of each other's injuries. We were like a convention of the wounded.

Driving back in the middle of the night we all talked on and off. Not one of us were at our best. Fran was not with us. Apparently she could not yet face her father. Paula had come over to collect her and she would be staying in London for a while. I hoped it wouldn't be too long a while.

Somewhere around Leicester Debra exclaimed:

"My car! I've left my car down there!"

"I'll buy you a new one, babe." I slapped my pocket "Still got some change from the painkillers."

Kelp roared. Debra was silent. But I like to think she was laughing on the inside.

Monday afternoon. After almost a full Sunday of sleeping and being purred at, I had driven over to Manchester with Tim to visit Mark's mother. I had phoned her that morning and tried to give her the story of how her son's killers were to be bought to justice. She'd wanted me to come over. I'd roped Tim in too as a representative of Club Zed. He needed some closure on all this as sure as Mrs. Fawcett did. Tim was carrying a bouquet of flowers almost bigger than himself, bought from a whip-round amongst club staff. He kept trying to palm them off onto me but I told him they'd strain my ribs.

We sat on the sofa after introductions. Tim acted all shy for some reason and seemed to forget to offer the flowers. They just about obscured him as he sat there, peeking out from behind them. I didn't think it my place to prompt.

Mark's funeral had taken place whilst I was away in Dorset and I told Anna that I wished I could have been there. Anna said it was okay and then added, "I spoke to Barry on the phone this lunchtime. He said he was sorry he couldn't be here to meet you. He told me to tell you he owes you one."

I nodded. Anna smiled.

"Now, tea." She said fairly brightly and went off into the kitchen. When she was gone Tim turned to me and said, "Barry? Is that Mr. Fawcett then?"

"No, that's Mark's brother. He's away with the army."

Tim seemed pleased about that. I gave him a look.

"Always good when someone with weapons training says they owe you one," he explained.

"Tim..."

"What?"

"When she comes back, give her the fucking flowers, yeah?"

She came back with the tea and biscuits. Tim performed a mumbling presentation of the bouquet and she seemed genuinely touched.

"They're beautiful! I must get a vase for them," said Anna and bustled off into the kitchen again.

Her eyes were wet but she wasn't crying.

Whilst she was gone Tim turned to me again and said, "No Mr. Fawcett?"

"No, Tim. She doesn't trust men."

He nodded solemnly. It was really quite amusing.

When Anna came back through with the vase you could tell Tim wanted to say something but didn't know what.

"Nice vase," he came up with.

Anna smiled a thank you as she placed them on the front window sill and I did my best not to snigger. God, was I going to rib him about this later. The vase was plastic and probably from Poundstretcher. Then the fates drew Tim's eye to a row of LPs in one of those old stereo cabinets.

"Is that the Dean Martin boxed set?" he asked her. Anna had sat down opposite us by now and nodded enthusiastically.

"I'm his biggest fan. I've got all the CDs and albums. Do you like him?"

"He's all I listen to. Apart from Frank of course, but Dino's my favourite," replied Tim.

"I can actually vouch for that, Anna. He was playing in the car all the way over," I said, but no one was listening to me. Anna was rapt.

"I saw him in Vegas once," continued Tim.

Anna's jaw nearly hit the carpet. Her moist eyes widened and for a split second she didn't look a day over eighteen. Tim launched into an animated run down of the set list and special guest stars. I knew when I wasn't wanted.

"Anna. Take care. I'll be in touch. Tim, I'm off to the Village for a drink with my poofy friends, I'll make my own way back, I'll see you later."

No one was listening. I let myself out.

That's *amoure*.

The following evening we had an invite to go over to Trevini's. Me, Debra and Kelp that is. I drove us in Debra's Micra, her wrist was still out of action. One of the Dorset Constabulary had kindly driven her car up for her on the Monday. It would have got them out of regular duties for a whole two shifts I suppose. We were starting to sense something like a grudging respect from the police by then. Even the Bradford Squad. Hadley had phoned and told me he wasn't planning to press any obstruction charges. I asked if this meant he'd be sending a Christmas card but he'd hung up by then.

Evie excelled herself with the catering and Tim looked the happiest I'd seen him for a long time. Trevini still had a weight on his shoulders but looked after us so well. At one point he was away talking to Fran on the phone. I came with him to his study. There was not much proper conversation and what was said sounded strained. But at least they were talking.

Trevini then handed me the phone and went back to the dining room. Fran started to say hello but then just began sobbing. She kept repeating "I'm sorry." And I kept saying it was okay. Eventually I took the initiative and hung up.

Back at the dining table the Chianti flowed and so did our emotions. Mostly laughter but some tears. Much later, Trevini said he had something to show us. We were led through the kitchen and pantry and then a quarry-tiled corridor that linked to a large garage. Gleaming like polished onyx was a black Ford Escort. Just like my old car, alloys and everything, but newer and cleaner.

"This is for you, Chris," said Trevini proudly.

He knew I considered the Focus to be ugly so he'd managed to find one of the last model Escorts for me. It was a 16 valve S-reg. It had one previous owner, air conditioning and a quarter of my old mileage on the clock.

Boy, did I hug him.

I said this meant I wouldn't be invoicing him for my work. He said that I would and that also he would be paying me the reward that was offered in the paper. I said there was no way. Kelp looked like he wanted to kick me but couldn't because of his pot.

Eventually I settled on the car, two weeks doorman's wages and the reward to be split between Debra and Kelp.

Back at the table once more, we were on to coffees and

brandies. I was tugging on a big fat cigar too. Kelp had gone through to the games room and was shooting zombies on House of the Dead. If I knew him, he was already mentally spending his half of the reward too. I glanced out of the window and saw that it was snowing. The first of the season. Large perfect flakes swirling like feathers in the night air.

Debra's hand was in mine and we excused ourselves from the table.

"You are not driving home. I will call a taxi or you will stay here," said Trevini.

"We'll stay tonight if that's okay. We're just going for a walk."

We crunched along the gravel driveway, arm in arm and pressed up against each other, taking slow steps. We crossed the road and walked up through the woods until Ilkley Moor came into view, then we just stood and watched the landscape becoming white and clean around us.

We kissed, with the full blessing of the moon above.

"Debra?"

"O'Brien?"

"What are you doing for Christmas?"

"You, babe. You," she replied.

We kissed and kissed again.